The Scavenger's Tale

The taller Monitor placed her hand on my shoulder.

'You can't,' I squealed. 'My family's opted out.'

'Nobody opts out, pet. Every human being has the potential to offer the gift of life to another. Now take it easy. Just a little shot. A nice sedative.' She took the sterile wrapping off a syringe-pak while the other held me . . .

It is 2015, after the great Conflagration, and London has become a tourist sight for people from all over the world, coming to visit the historic Heritage Centres. These are out of bounds to people like Bedford and his sister Dee who live in an Unapproved Temporary Dwelling and have to scavenge from skips and bins just to stay alive.

Bedford begins to notice something odd about the tourists: when they arrive in the city, they are desperately ill, but when they leave they seem to have been miraculously cured. And then the Dysfuncs start disappearing. It is only when a stranger appears, terribly injured, that Bedford begins to put two and two together . . .

RACHEL ANDERSON was born in 1943 at Hampton Court. She and her husband, who teaches drama, have a daughter and three sons. She has worked in radio and newspaper journalism and in 1991 won the Medical Journalists' Association Award. She has written four books for adults, though now writes mostly for children. She won the Guardian Children's Fiction Award in 1992 for *Paper Faces*. When not writing, she is involved with the needs and care of children who are socially or mentally challenged.

The Scavenger's Tale

THE
SCAVENGER'S
TALE

Rachel Anderson

OXFORD
UNIVERSITY PRESS

OXFORD
UNIVERSITY PRESS

Great Clarendon Street, Oxford OX2 6DP

Oxford University Press is a department of the University of Oxford.
It furthers the University's objective of excellence in research, scholarship,
and education by publishing worldwide in

Oxford New York

Athens Auckland Bangkok Bogotá Buenos Aires Calcutta
Cape Town Chennai Dar es Salaam Delhi Florence Hong Kong Istanbul
Karachi Kuala Lumpur Madrid Melbourne Mexico City Mumbai
Nairobi Paris São Paulo Singapore Taipei Tokyo Toronto Warsaw

and associated companies in Berlin Ibadan

Oxford is a registered trade mark of Oxford University Press
in the UK and in certain other countries

Copyright © Rachel Anderson 1998

The moral rights of the author have been asserted

First published 1998
First published in this paperback edition 2000

1 3 5 7 9 10 8 6 4 2

British Library Cataloguing in Publication Data available

ISBN 0 19 275022 4

Typeset by AFS Image Setters Ltd, Glasgow
Printed in Great Britain by
Cox & Wyman Ltd, Reading, Berkshire

For Dorothy, who goes on caring

1

In the Beginning There Was

A few weeks back, there was an ugly incident at school. It involved one of my sisters, my primo favourite kid sister, Devonshire. We call her Dee. She isn't very old, she isn't very smart, and she doesn't communicate too well.

'Den dey come along, come along hop-along, hip-along,' she was saying. Dee had such a funny sing-song way of talking. 'Den grabbit rabbit! Hop-along!'

Then something about 'the pool'. She was upset about it. Being agitated doesn't help her talk sense either.

'Try and talk more slowly, Dee,' I said.

'Den dis away, dat away, down. Dey pool. Dey pool.'

'Pool?' I said. 'What pool? Funny bunny rabbits took you to a swimming pool?'

Not that any of us can swim. There's no leisure pools open to ordinary citizens round here, though there used to be a public one over on High Holborn. But that's been upgraded for tourists. Then there's the water fountains in Trafalgar Square. But I don't suppose Dee meant those. We're not supposed to hang out round there. That's tourist territory too, strictly off-limits.

I was tired of hearing about her bunny rabbits. 'Give it a rest, Dee,' I said. I was busy trying to manoeuvre us safely across Shaftesbury Avenue without being knocked down by taxis, limos, or pedicabs.

We passed the Mikado South-East Asian takeaway. London City Sector One caters for all sorts of foreign tastes. Visitors like such weird things. On the Mikado menu, they've got octopus, honey-roast locusts, barbecue dog-ribs. Makes you hungry just walking past and sniffing the air.

Dee wouldn't let her story drop. She was burbling on about tea. I guess she was hungry.

'So you and your rabbits were down at the pool and had tea?' I said tetchily.

'No, no, no!' She seemed desperate. 'Real! Make it real. Not glory-story tell Tale-times.'

She meant that she was trying to tell me about something that'd actually happened. It wasn't supposed to be one of her long-winded fairy tales.

So taking tea with bunny rabbits was out. It wasn't 'tea' she was on about but 'T-shirt', only she'd forgotten, in her anxiety, to add the 'shirt' part. And she didn't mean 'rabbit' either, but 'grab it'. Her frustration at my slowness increased. Suddenly, outside the big plate-glass shop window filled with the gold and diamond watches that the tourists come over here to buy, she pulled up her little black vest and showed me her scraggy chicken chest. It was bruised. And her arms.

'So your class went on a trip to a pool and you tripped over?' I suggested though it seemed about as unlikely as the bunnies. We never go on trips. We're not allowed outside our Sector.

'No, no, no!' she was crying with distress. 'Dey pull, dey pull.'

The swimming pool was a false lead too. She didn't mean 'the pool' but 'they pull'. Somebody had pulled her. And quite roughly by the look of it.

So when did this happen? In the school yard? During classtime? And who was it?

From her garbled account, it seemed that at some point during the day somebody, or perhaps several naughty somebodies, had tried to grab her and pull her where she didn't want to go. All the way home, she stuck to the same story. Dee's memory was good. She just didn't have enough language skill to express what she saw, meant, thought. So what was it all about? Why would anybody deliberately want to hurt a little girl with slanty eyes?

Probably one of the bigger boys. They might've been jealous. The fact is, my sister Devonshire is a Dysfunc. Not that this matters to us at home. I have a dysfunctional elder brother too. And my newest sister, Netta, is dysfunctional with CP. That's cerebral palsy. It means she was damaged at birth, though not on purpose. In fact, I'm the only person in our family who hasn't got a profound impairment.

When Dee first started coming along to the Windmill Street school, the teachers treated her differently. A few made allowances. Others watched her warily. Did they think she might grow fangs and bite?

Our Ma Peddle was steaming cross when she heard about the bruising on Dee's body, as though Dee getting caught in the middle of rough boys' horseplay was my fault.

'That's not fair!' I said.

'You knows what I mean,' Our Ma Peddle snapped. 'You got to take better care of them that can't care for themselves.'

But how could I keep watching out for her when I was in my own class? 'I haven't got eyes in the back of my head,' I muttered.

Our Ma Peddle decided to kick up a fuss with school.

'When we sends our precious little ones to a seat of learning, what we expects is how they'll be safe from harm,' she said. She wasn't to know that, for a child like Dee, there wasn't any place that was safe from harm, not in City Sector One anyhow.

Our Ma Peddle reckoned that Dysfunctionals and Abs had the same basic right to education, food, justice, as every other citizen. Some hope.

Our Ma Peddle wanted help with a letter to the school Director. I wasn't too keen. It was going to be dead

3

tricky if one small bullying incident got turned into a mega discipline issue, specially if whoever roughed Dee up turned out to be one of my own mates. I even had an idea who it might be. Callam. Sometimes he can be really rough, like he owns the world, just because he lives in a posh flat.

I knew that when the Director mentioned the accident during Roll-Call, everybody would turn and stare. First at me, then at Dee. We get enough of that out on the streets. Because of her condition, which is called the Doctor John Langdon Down Syndrome, or DJLDS, she's quite distinctive.

Foreign tourists stare and point all the time. Maybe they don't have people like her in their countries. Once, a smart lady leaned out of the side of a pedicab and spat at us. I wanted to remind her that spitting and sneezes spread diseases, especially tuberculosis. But, of course, Dee and I are far more likely to be disease-carriers than a fine rich visitor from afar, staying in one of the grand hotels.

In fact, to my relief, at Roll-Call, the Director never mentioned Dee's unhappy incident. But he must have passed the message on to the Sector Governors. Ages after Dee's bruises had faded, Our Ma Peddle got a letter, official-looking, hand-delivered by the courier.

I read it out to her.

Madam

An alleged incident of bullying, reputedly involving one of your surrogate children, by a citizen or citizens unknown, was reported. An investigation was undertaken. To date, your allegations have not been substantiated.

Pupil problems occurring outside school attendance hours are outwith our jurisdiction. They should be reported to the Community Street

4

Wardens on form CD/62/BAC, obtainable from your local council office.

However, recent reports of street unruliness in City Sector One have been greatly exaggerated. We would remind you that malicious gossip, scandal-mongering, and the spread of false rumour are all offences under the Good Citizenship Regulation (2012), and subject to a Caution.

'Bad bad bad thing!' Dee said importantly when I'd finished reading the letter out to Our Ma Peddle. Dee understood that it concerned her and that she was, briefly, the centre of family attention.

'Yes, my pet,' said Our Ma Peddle. 'But it won't go happening again, not if you be a good girl, and always do what you're told.'

She really thought it wouldn't happen again. So did I, specially after I'd given Callam a firm rebuke about bullying.

'Dunno what you're on about,' he said.

Dee may not always know how many beans make five, but she has a memory for faces. And it seems it wasn't Callam's face that haunted her.

We were walking home when two Community Health and Welfare Monitors leaped out of their white CareCar just ahead of us. They were tall and fair with the clear kindly eyes of all the Community Health and Welfare Monitors in our Sector. One of them carried the paramedic case they always have and they went dashing down the road to sort out some smelly old drunk who'd fallen into the gutter. I don't know why they bothered. He looked to me like he was already a stiff.

Dee pointed. 'Dem!' she said. 'Dere dem! Dey pull. Dey pull. Bully pully!'

'Don't point like that,' I whispered. 'You know courtesy counts.'

It's one of the Good Citizen Regs. You can get a serious Caution for being offensive to any of our community workers.

So Dee tried to point discreetly, nodding her dainty pixie nose in the direction of the two lithe nurses in their white action suits. They crouched over the old man. They undid his shirt. They pressed the stethoscope to his chest.

'Dat dem, dey pull, grab me! Bad bad bad!' Dee whispered. 'Grabbit pully bully! Ow ow ow!'

She seemed to think that the stethoscope on the man's ribs was hurting him.

'No, silly. They're listening to his heart. Checking it's beating OK.'

We watched while the two Community Health and Welfare Monitors heaved the old fellow on to a stretcher, slid him into the back of their CareCar and sped off through the traffic, siren wailing.

'Bad girls!' Dee insisted.

'Don't be daft. They're not bad,' I said. 'CHAWMs are kind paramedics who help to keep us fit and well. We're lucky to have such a good health care system.'

Back then, I believed it.

2

Where is Dee's ID?

Straight after school, I wanted to go on a quick scavvy. Round the back-courts. Behind Piccadilly. Off Leicester Square, Covent Garden. City Sector One's primo if you want quality scavvies. Hotels throw out loads of stuff for recycling.

I decided to take Dee with me. She's growing up fast. She shouldn't stay in the flat so much. She's been on at me. Every time she sees me going out on some errand, even if it's only down to the standpipe with the bucket. But Our Ma Peddle worries in case Dee gets us into trouble with the Community Street Wardens. In truth, it's not Dee she thinks will do something bad. It's me. Our Ma Peddle trusts me about as much as a hole in the head.

'Me too, me too, Bedford!' Dee nagged. 'Pleeeeease? Wanna come with you. I'm big. I'm ten. Twenty ten thousand!'

'No, Dee, you're too young.'

'Ten is a big-wig. See me count to ten!' She held up her chubby little hands and wiggled her stubby fingers at me to show she knew about counting. 'Ten, nine, six, seven, three, two, one.'

Her slanting piggy eyes were peeking out, shiny bright, beneath the heavy folds of the upper lids. They're epicanthal. It says so on her ID, under 'distinguishing features'.

Her fleshy drooping lips lifted in a pleading smile. She looks like a short elf, and I really rate her. I'll do anything for her.

'Me too, Bedford, take me!'

She's right. She needs to learn scavenging skills. I'd

begun watching out for myself long before I was her age. But then *I* began doing loads of stuff which Dee'll never do. I may be classified as Low-Caste, but I'm not one of the defectively-abled. I'm High Intelligence Quotient.

But if Dee comes, then lanky Rah has to come too. You can't leave a beanpole boy to find his own way home. He'd never make it. Sometimes Rajah gets lost just trying to find his way out of his vest. He'll holler and struggle till someone helps him to the safe exit for his two arms.

Besides, although he's daft, he's strong. If we find anything big, I'll need him to carry it. I definitely want us to find something primo, *bueno*, first chop, which Our Ma Peddle really likes so she'll be pleased with me for a change instead of moaning that I'm a dead weight on family life.

OK, so I *know* I should've walked them both back to the flat first, got them safely in, given them a drink of water to keep their bellies quiet, then gone out again after that.

It was a quiet afternoon. A few jet-lagged Pacific Rimmers shuffled about in their tour group taking snaps of anything that moved. No serious signs of agitation from our local coven of vagrants and misfits. And even if there were, the Community Street Wardens would soon sort them out for us. That's what the CSWs are for. So I reckoned there was no harm in it. Give Our Ma Peddle a bit of peace and quiet to put her feet up.

At breaktime we're sent out into the exercise yard. I went over to the Junior's corner where Dee was playing knuckle-stones on the dirt-ground with her pals. Although her hands look an odd shape, they're dexterous.

'A scavvy. After school today,' I told her. 'You can come too. But you've got to do everything I say. That

8

means, stick close, not touch a thing that you find without asking me first. Because there's sometimes some very nasty things.'

I didn't spell out *what* nasty things. But she probably knew anyway. You see them sticking out of garbage, even in the skips right outside hotels. Needles and razor blades, broken dentures, bits of dead dog. She may be retarded but somehow she wasn't exactly stupid.

'Do you understand?'

'Yes-yes-yes, yessy yes. How many any more times I have to say it?' She was always mimicking our speech.

'Really understand? So what have I just said?'

That's Our Ma Peddle's trick, making her repeat back instructions to make sure she's cottoned on.

'Not touchy touch. Ask big brother first.' She stretched her short arms round my waist and hugged. 'Bedford, my best boy. Love you I do.'

I like to believe she was nearly as fond of me as I was of her, even though some people say that the Abnormals aren't capable of true feelings.

At the end of the day, I waited at the Junior's door. Her friends greeted me as they streamed into the yard. I'm in Middle School now. They get crushes on me. I hate that kind of thing.

'Hi there, Bedford. Your sister's just coming.'

Although her friends were mainstreamers, they took care of her. *They* didn't seem to think she had no feelings. Dee was the only Dysfunc in her class.

'Got your snackbox, Dee?' I asked when she emerged last of all. Her stumpy legs don't find stairs easy.

'Yup.' She handed it over for me to carry. I lifted the lid and peered in to check she'd actually eaten something during the day.

'Good girl,' I said for she'd eaten more than half her

9

pouch of pitta bread. It was stuffed with grated raw turnip. We have to make sure Dee eats properly.

When Our Ma Peddle first found her on Devonshire Place, she was no more than a scraggy bag of bones. I was only young but I still remember. Ma Peddle had to coax her with warm mush on a teaspoon, just so she'd stay alive.

'Got your track-shoes?' I said briskly. Windmill Street Community School has never had sports facilities. We still have to bring in full kit in case there's a Governor's Inspection.

Dee nodded, and handed over her never-worn spike-shoes for me to carry.

'Think I'm your servant or something?' I said. I always carry her stuff anyway. She's small for her age, she tires easily. Sometimes she goes blue. She has a heart condition as well as everything else, poor little mite.

I said, 'And your ID?'

She looked blank.

'Your little yellow card?'

No. She hadn't got it. At any rate, we couldn't find it in any of her pockets. Perhaps she'd dropped it. Or left it on the teacher's work station. She grinned. Perhaps she doesn't yet understand the new regulation, that we have to carry them at all times. Ma Peddle hung Rah's round his neck on a string. I persuaded her that it's undignified to make Dee do that.

'Dee's not that dim,' I said. Seems like I was wrong. Better to be undignified than picked up on the street without your ID, and escorted off to some distant Classification Centre in Hounslow. To get a replacement, you have to spend days queuing and form-filling. And if there's any likelihood that you might be one of the Abs or Dysfuncs you're put through Classification all over again.

'In the classy classroom?' Dee suggested hopefully. 'Maybe, maybe, that's where. On the pesky desky desk?'

So we went to search. Wasting precious time when we could have been scavenging.

'You must never put it down, Dee. Are you listening? You must always keep it with you. It's even more important than your spikes, or your snackbox.'

I nagged on at her, just like Our Ma Peddle, all the way up three flights of stairs. Our school was built tall and thin like all the other buildings on Windmill Street. It must be very old. The figure 1883 is carved into a plaque on the side, though that could be a fake for the tourists.

Since 1883, there have been over three hundred major Conflagrations. In those days though, they used to call them war. Later, they called them conflict, then civil unrest. The effect was always the same. People killed each other in order to get more food, or power, or land, or a little bit of ocean.

'OK, OK, I heard,' Dee said. She was puffing and blue round the lips by the time we reached the end of the top corridor.

I shouldn't have been so sharp. She couldn't help being a Dysfunc with Low Intelligence Quotient. In truth, I was annoyed with her teacher. You'd think they'd bother to check that a kid like Dee had her ID before sending her home. Maybe the teacher didn't like having a Dysfunc mixed up with mainstreamers. Some people minded. Some didn't.

Our janitor was already up there, dragging the vacuum aspirator across the classroom. He was getting on a bit, could hardly hold the nozzle steady in his knobbly hands. And there, on the floor, lay the bright yellow plastic of somebody's dropped ID.

'Please, Mr Winkins, sir!' I yelled. 'Stop! Down there! Look!'

Over the throb of the cleaner, he didn't hear. Any moment now, that ID's going to be sucked away to oblivion.

In two ticks, I was skidding on my belly across the tops of the desks, diving to the floor, snatching the card to safety.

It was hers all right.

> *Abnormalities*: Trisomy 21. 47th Chromosome
> *Prevailing Condition*: Doctor John Langdon Down Syndrome (DJLDS)
> *Code*: 4590BN7888MNS349/B
> *Distinguishing Features*: epicanthal folds
> *Appearance*: high-grade mongol
> *Address*: Unapproved Temporary Dwelling Place no. 624/11 BAGF, Whitcomb Street, Leicester Square, London City Sector 1.
> *Anticipated date of expiry*: 01/01/2015.
> *Issuing Office*: Ministry of Public Information.

Mr Winkins looked startled. He hadn't even realized we were there.

'Got it!' I said waving the card to show him what I was about. 'Just in time!'

He shook his head slowly. His eyes were clouded over with a film of sadness.

I wasn't to know that this was the last time I'd get to speak to him. If I'd known what was going to happen, I'd definitely have said a bit more than just, 'Goodnight, sir.'

He was back to his vacuuming so he didn't hear.

'Goodnight, goody night, stinky wrinkly Winky!' shouted Dee. 'See you in morning. See you!'

Mr Janitor Winkins, I hope that whatever remains of you now is resting in the Place of Peace, wherever that might be.

3

How We Found Rah's Man

We crossed the exercise yard to pick up Rah from the
SWU. That's the Special Works Unit on the other side.
I explained to him carefully that we weren't going
home.

'Not right away. So you got to keep close and not do
anything dappy. OK, pal?'

He brayed. I'm not sure he understood. He's four
years older than me but he's never going to add up to
much. I think his brain's about as big as a pigeon's. In
the SWU they make the older Dysfuncs sort metal nuts
and screws. They're from defused landmines. They get
re-used for something else. Even sorting screws taxes
Rah's tiny pigeon brain to its limit.

Dee skipped excitedly beside me. 'Hold you hand,
Bedford? Hold?' she begged.

Rah staggered along behind on his ungainly beanpole
legs like a man on stilts.

Because of that silly search for Dee's ID, by the time
we got going most of the decent stuff had gone. But I
still got that buzz. Like the start of an adventure story.
When you set out on a scavvy, you never know what
might turn up. Mostly, nothing. Just occasionally, you
hit the jackpot.

We stopped to sift through refuse behind the Strand
Palace Hotel. The skips are stencilled on the outside,
RECYCLING CENTRE. The main recycling gets done
by keen private enterprisers like me and Dee and Rah.
We were just moving on to the next one when a long
limo with smoky-blue rear windows went slinking by.
Foreign tourists spending loads of dosh. So we bowed
and smiled in the approved way.

'*Bonjour. Shalom. Assalam alaikum.* G'day.' Doesn't matter what you say so long as you say it nicely.

However irritating things are with the shortages, I always love that mood out on the streets as the evening's entertainment starts hotting up. Even if you can't join in, it's primo just to know it's there. I reckon we're dead lucky to live at the centre of the civilized world.

In the next skip, I found a strip of broken shelving and an empty army boot. Sometimes you find them with a foot still inside.

Our Ma Peddle was hardly going to say 'Whoopee' about either of these. I tossed them both back.

Dee pounced on a hand of soft black bananas. I told her she should share them with Rah.

'Ooh thanky thank you, Bedford!' she said, grateful. Already, this educational walkabout was well up to her expectations.

'I tell you what!' I said. 'Let's nip down to the river. Just check it out.'

Our Ma Peddle doesn't like me going there because of the water-borne diseases. But it's such an ace place for a scavvy.

The Thames is neutral, a no man's land between the sectors. If Dee or I were ever in trouble, I reckon that's where we'd go. City Sector One ends at the Embankment wall. The next sector, South Sector Three, doesn't start till over on the far bank. Some days the river's so full it looks as though you could walk right across on the skin of floating stuff. When tides and winds are right, it washes ashore. Mostly useless bits but occasionally there's treasure. That's how I found our bench, a curtain, and a mattress for Netta. One time, I saw someone pick up a whole crateful of some foreign product. PINEAPPLES SIERRA LEONE was branded on the side.

We crossed the cobbled forecourt of the Charing Cross terminus.

'Long way, long,' said Dee, puffing.

'Not much further. Nearly there,' I lied. I knew I'd already made her walk too far. But it'd be a crying shame not to take a peek by the river. I hurried us down Villiers Street where it's dark and slippery. The Community Street Wardens don't like coming down here so it doesn't get cleared very often. But it's not a historic tourist area so it doesn't matter.

We had to get past the drunks burping and lounging in their huddle under the bridge. The CS Wardens ought to do something about them.

When we reached Embankment, I scrambled on to the wall, hauled Dee and Rah after me, and helped them slither down the other side. They landed on the narrow bank of silty mud. Quite a decent lot of garbage today. But you have to tread gently. Nestling in amongst domestic refuse, there's often armaments rusting, holsters, broken Kalashnikovs. Never any ammunition. That was scavenged ages ago.

The tide was flowing swiftly out. The water's always thick khaki-coloured.

'Keep away from the edge,' I ordered Rah. 'Please,' I added, for I try to teach him street manners in case he's ever picked on by a CSW.

As usual, too late. He saw those slappy little waves. He lurched forward and went in knee-deep, laughing with delight. He could scarcely keep his balance in the current. Rah loved water. He didn't know it was full of cholera and stuff.

I yelled. 'Get out, you big baboon! Come back over here. It's dangerous.'

I don't know why I bothered. It's up to *me* to watch out for *him*. He can't swim. He doesn't understand hot or cold, let alone wet or danger. He looked down at his disappeared legs, mystified as to where they'd gone. He chuckled. He was happy.

15

I grabbed his arm, yanked him back to stand against the embankment wall. I should be gentle with him. It's not his fault.

Dee and I got busy scrabbling through the tangle of stuff. I showed her how to do it. She's not bad at learning if you explain clearly. I noticed something bright and shiny. I made a grab for it, just as I'd been telling Dee you never should. I thought it was a decorated glass dish. I had it in mind to find something nice for Our Ma Peddle, to win her approval. But when I pulled, out came a fragment of aviation steel. It ripped my hand. I moved to another pile. Again, nothing useful except for a supershopper trolley. Our Ma Peddle's already got three of them.

'Nothing doing, Dee. We better be pushing home.'

'Nevvy mind. Betty lucky nother time,' she agreed.

I called to Rah. 'Come on, Rajah Peddle.'

He ignored me.

'Rah, we're going back. Now! I don't know about you, but I'm ready for tea.'

He squatted near the wall. I thought he must be sulking about his wet trouser legs.

'Rah,' I said. 'Come *on*!'

He was poking with a little stick. He'd found a scavvy in a great heap of mess. Poke, prod, poke, he went.

Dee and I went to look. It was organic, a sea creature of some kind, slimy with mud, very dead. Rah kept on worrying at its eyes.

'Don't, Rah. That's nasty.'

'Yeah. Nasty nasty boy, you.' Dee snatched Rah's poking stick from him and had a go herself at the dark eyes sunk in the skull.

Suddenly she yelped, 'Man!' She stopped poking. 'Rah got a manny man!'

She was right. The face was dirty and bearded so that it didn't look quite human. The rest of it was buried in

16

rubbish. Perhaps a drunken sailor who'd taken a tot too many and tumbled overboard. Or a vagrant who'd got in a fight. Not long dead from the smell of it. Corpses begin to smell sickly sweet after a while. This one smelled sweaty and unwashed.

With any luck, no one had scavenged it yet. Even a vagrant had a ration book. Or there might be an ID. Spares are always handy. You can alter the info on an ID to suit your own needs.

'Man,' said Rah clearly. 'Mine.' He doesn't often speak.

'Yes. Well done, Rah,' I said. 'Good scavvy you got us.'

He looked pleased, though less so when I pushed him aside so I could go through the clothing.

'Don't keep poking,' I told Dee. '*Search* it. In the pockets. See what's there. It's all right. It won't bite. It's dead.'

Rah crouched down too and began picking shreds of rotting fabric off the stiff's jacket, popping them into his mouth and chewing. Rah was always hungry but had no discrimination however hard we tried to teach him.

Others must have scavvied ahead of us. There were seven pockets, all empty, except the last one which had a scrap of card, scribbled with lines and a few words which didn't mean anything to me, and a small knife. This was a lot more interesting. It had a red handle marked with a white cross. I recognized the type from pictures we'd been shown at school by the Community Security Squad of anti-personnel weapons we have to be on the alert for. Hidden inside the knife's red handle are twenty or more different blades and instruments. The CSS call it the Swiss Army Knife. It could be useful. I wondered why no previous scavenger had taken it. Perhaps they were looking for something specific. I

17

wanted to keep the knife. But if it was found on me, I'd be in even worse trouble than not having my ID.

'Not dead,' said Dee. 'Manny's gone sleepybyes.'

'Don't be an idiot, Dee!' I snapped. 'People don't sleep with their eyes open. Even you know that.'

Yes, I know I shouldn't call her an idiot when in fact she comes into the Classification of High-Grade Cretin. But I get impatient when I reckon she's not being as sensible as she could. Also, I was peeved that our scavvy was turning out to be useless.

'He not sleepy hush-a-bye no more,' Dee persisted. 'Look, Bedford. He's say wakey-wakey now.' She gave another prod with her chubby index finger at the skin stretched across the cheeks. The body started. The staring eyes snapped shut, then wide open again.

The mouth of the body sighed softly. 'Help me, boy. Help me.'

A living man! This was the best find of all. I'd never brought anything like this home. Our Ma Peddle would be really proud of me. We'd saved someone in need.

'Lend a hand, can't you, Rah?' I said. 'I can't lift him on my own.'

Dee said indignantly, 'He call me "boy". I not "boy". I slender gender, female.'

This wasn't the moment to discuss Classification. 'Just get out of the way so Rah can help,' I snapped.

Rah's Man was too heavy to haul over the embankment wall. We had to roll him on to a strip of tarpaulin, then drag the makeshift sledge along the river bank to where there's a flight of stone steps. They're green and slimy. He cried out when we bumped him up. Rah and Dee stood guard against rivals while I dashed back to fetch the discarded supershopper trolley from the garbage pile.

This was Rah's Man so I let him do the pushing. I carried Dee piggyback. We'd been out longer than I meant. I kept an eye out for CS Wardens. They'd be bound to stop us and go through the ID rigmarole. But they were busy in the railway terminus rounding up vagrants.

We reached home. The flat was damp and steamy. I love that swampy smell. The promise of boiled vegetables. We were lucky. There was a meal.

However, Our Ma Peddle was half-hysterical.

'Where in heck you lot been?' she yelled. That was before she'd seen what we'd heaved through the main gate and up the stairs. When I unwrapped the greasy tarpaulin and showed her our gift, she went ape with anger.

'Man,' said Rah excitedly. 'Man man.' It was good he'd started to speak. A pity that it wasn't more varied.

4

How Our Ma Peddle
Received Her Gift

'So what in heck do I need with an old drunk?' she
screeched.

'He's not old,' I said.

You couldn't tell, slumped on the tarpaulin in the
passageway.

'Not just drunk but stinking like bad fish.' She
prodded the body with her big bare toe, then went back
to stirring the soup on the stove.

'Well, you ain't leaving it there. You'll have to be rid
of it before I starts tripping over it.'

'But, Ma, we can't put him out. He's *human*!' She's
always on about the value of every single life, even the
drunks and vagrants, how we must share our last sou
and crumb with someone in a less fortunate position for
we might find ourselves stuck up the same alley some
day.

'Verminous, carrying cholera and goodness knows
what else,' she nagged as she tipped more water on to
the chopped vegetables in the big black pot. Water
makes soup go further. Even though she has precious
little sight, she has a creepy way of knowing exactly
where you are. I wouldn't dare slip away till she gave
permission.

'As though I haven't enough on my plate. He's
probably armed. And going to leap up and slash us all to
bits as soon as he comes round.'

'No blades on him,' I lied. 'We searched. Honest. Tell
her, Dee. We didn't find anything, did we?'

But Dee was too blue to speak. If I felt bad, it wasn't
about bringing in this misjudged gift. Nor about telling
a fib. It was about keeping Dee outside too long. 'Listen,

Ma,' I said, 'he might turn out to be really useful. He could work for you. Be like your very own domestic personnel.'

'We don't hold with no forced labour plans, as you well know.'

'Non-paying lodger, then? Do the heavy stuff? Carry things for you? Mend the windows?'

'The Sector's coming to fix them any day now. And this here's just another mouth to feed. Hasn't come with a silver spoon in its mouth, I'll be bound. Let alone its own ration book.'

'You could send him out scavvying. Ahead of the rush. He could get to the good stuff.' I often thought about that crazy crate of Pineapples Sierra Leone and wondered what they were.

'I'd have thought you, of all people, Bedford Peddle, had a sight more sense. And as for taking Devonshire off like that. I really trusted you to be sensible. But sometimes I think you ought to be sent off for re-Classification.'

She didn't mean it. She hadn't the money. It costs a right packet to get re-Classified. People like us don't use cash. We get coupons to use at the Ration Exchange Centre.

Rah's Man tried to sit up and his tattered gabardine fell open. I saw a flash of cotton undergarment. It was scarlet like he was a leaking beetroot.

Our Ma Peddle was right. We should've left him. He was terminally wounded.

'Ma,' I said. 'There's something else. There's a little bit of leakage on him.'

'And where's that?'

'On his side. Low down.' Sometimes, however annoyed with her you are, you have to tell her things or she wouldn't know. 'Like a small nick.' Actually, I could see it was a fine big gaping gash, like he'd been slashed apart so someone could search inside.

21

In an instant, Our Ma Peddle was down there on her knees, feeling him, searching for his head, pushing away the matted hair to stroke his brow. For a big woman, she's gentle. Then her hands were searching his body to find the injury.

'So what's up with you then, my poor old matey?' she murmured. 'Where does it hurt? You tell your Ma about it.'

It's nice when you hear Our Ma Peddle talking soft. I moved closer. But she sensed I was there at her elbow.

'It's not *you* I'm speaking to,' she snapped. 'You can take your soup and be off to your bed. And stay there till I tell you otherwise. Though before you go, you can do something useful for a change. Fetch us up water. Put it on to heat. I'll need to get this lot sluiced out, poor fellow.'

To the man, she said kindly, 'You can stay for tonight. But I ain't keeping you no longer.'

Obediently, I trogged down to the standpipe. Our flat's on the top floor, right under the roof-space, warm in summer, cool in winter. Sixty-four steps each way, lugging a bucket in each hand. By the time I was back and had set the pan on the stove, Our Ma Peddle had her hands scrubbed and was busying with swabs and salt solution and strips of torn sheeting. The man would be washed, then mended by the kindest pair of hands in the whole of City Sector One. If anyone could save him, she could.

'One more thing,' she said. 'This evening, no Tale-Times for you.'

She really knew how to make it hurt. To ban me from Tale-Times was mean.

'But, Ma, that's not *fair*,' I wailed. She knew I loved Tale-Times.

'Nothing ain't been fair since time began. Sooner you learn that, happier you'll be.'

As she started her repairs, the man's face twisted in pain so I didn't moan at my Ma any more. I filled my mug and slunk away to my bunk.

There's no light in the back room. It's cramped, stacked with old army bunk-beds. I share with Rah. There's cardboard tacked over the window-frames to stop Rah hurting himself on the jagged edges. Our block's an Unapproved Temporary Dwelling Place so quite a lot of the windows are still broken. The Sector keeps promising to do repairs as soon as they have resources available. But the A-Classifieds always get their repairs done first.

Outside, arc lights lit up Leicester Square with evening blue moonlight. I folded back a corner of the cardboard so I could watch reflected light bounce off the building opposite while I ate my supper.

I take the top bunk, Rah the lower. He still wets himself. I'd never advise anyone to sleep below him.

Turnip and pitta bread soup is brownish-yellow, sloppy and slippery. Turnips were currently plentiful at the REC. The pitta bread's the leftovers from Dee's packed dinner. Nothing goes to waste.

Even though I was in disgrace, I enjoyed my soup. I picked out the nice turnip chunks to eat as I listened to the friendly sounds coming through the wall. The bench scraping on the floor, tin mugs rattling, Dee prattling on.

Then it went quiet. Ma was starting her Tale-Times. She can't see to read. So she makes up stories instead. Some of them are brilliant, about kings and lions, shooting stars, famines and splendid celebrations during years of plenty. Last week she told one about a man who was so afraid of a rumoured global flood that he built himself a wooden boat and loaded it with all the animals and plants he could find. He sailed off to find a new and better world. Sometimes I wish we could be like that. Me, Dee, Ma, Netta, and Rah.

Yesterday, Ma had begun a new story about a boy named Joseph. I wished I was destined for leadership like that. I was called Bedfordsbury after the back alley where I was found.

Joseph had eleven strong, older brothers who knew how to manage camels. The only brother I had was Rah who didn't know how to do anything. He was found eating paper tablecloths outside the Rajah Indian restaurant.

In Ma's story, Joseph's brothers turned mean and threw him into a pit. I enjoyed that bit. Like being banished to a dark room no bigger than a cupboard, with black mould on the walls. Sometimes when Rah's wet himself and he's shouting and flinging his arms about, I want to fling him into a pit.

I never feel that about Dee. Is it wrong to love one sibling so much more than another?

So would Joseph get out of the pit? I pressed my ear to the wall so I could catch the rest of the story. I heard the rise and fall of Our Ma Peddle's voice but I couldn't make sense of it. What a waste. I was the only one who really understood Tale-Times. Unless, perhaps, Rah's Man was listening? Tomorrow, after school, I'd ask him.

But next day, two unusual things happened. One weird, one sad. Both at school.

5

The Seven Sacred Parts
of Mr Winkins

The weird thing first. Dee, Rah, and I arrived at school and found it was thundering with construction workers. In their hard hats and steel-capped boots, in our exercise yard, on the parapets, along the fire-escapes, with rolls of steel mesh, welding equipment, hacksaws. All the time we were in class, we could see them strutting past the windows on scaffolding walkways, and hear them sawing and riveting and drilling.

By break-time, we could see what they were up to. Barricading us in. Turning our school into a fortress, just like in the olden days when people had conflagrations which lasted for a hundred years and they poured boiling oil over each other's heads.

Our exercise yard was even getting fencing over the top of it. 'So it looks like we're in a monkey-cage!' laughed Callam. He began hopping around yelping like some crazy ape.

The gate on to Windmill Street was reinforced with steel panels and spiky wire along the top. During Community Studies, I asked our teacher what she thought was going on.

'Security,' said Ms Reed.

Callam said, 'But, Miss, everybody knows there's nothing left to nick.'

We had no books, or chalk. Even the old video screen had gone.

'It's not security to property that the Director's concerned about. It's security to personnel. To protect those who need protecting. Now please, pupils, do let's get on with what we're here for.'

After Community Studies, we had an hour of Civic

25

Responsibility, Politics, and World Order to prepare us for our roles in the Sector when we're adult. And finally Logarithms all afternoon. Our Ma Peddle says that when she was young, they used to have stories out of books read aloud to them. Doesn't sound much like real work to me.

The sad thing that happened was to do with the janitor. We heard that he'd been discovered to be suffering from such profound hearing loss and generalized malaise that the CHAWMs had to be called in but there was nothing they could do to save him.

'Please, Miss. What's malaise?' Callam piped up.

'A state of non-specific bodily discomfort and non-well-being.'

Gossip is prohibited under the Good Citizenship Regulation (2012) so we weren't supposed to chat about Mr Winkins among ourselves. But at the end of the day there was an official announcement that Mr Winkins had indeed passed on through the Great Divide to the Place of Peace and the Director was having a Memorial Roll-Call. No more Logarithms. Instead, we filed down to the hall and stood to attention facing the Sector flag for the two-minute silence.

Then, the Director cleared his throat and began to speak.

'Junior Citizens, stand at ease,' he said. (Nobody ever stood easy in his presence.) 'We are gathered to reflect upon the exemplary life of Citizen Georgio Winkins, now tragically departed, that we may remember, honour, and respect him. A man who, with unstinting generosity even though he was from one of the Sector's lower Castes, offered himself up, even after life's end, to give a chance of enhanced living to so many others.'

The Director listed the parts that Mr Winkins had donated.

'The two corneas from his eyes, so that two sightless

citizens of worth will shortly be enabled to view afresh our wondrous world.'

I thought of Ma Peddle. If only we could get her on to a transplant list so she could have eyes that worked properly.

'Two kidneys, already speeding to two members of the City Sector One Council, who have been so cruelly suffering from renal failure. But who, thanks to the noble gesture of our humble janitor, will shortly be able to resume their important and active roles. One pancreas, one liver, one splendidly healthy heart, for the departed was not a smoker and had no history of hereditary heart disease. The ultimate destination of the other organs must remain undisclosed.' That meant they were destined for someone even more High Caste than a Sector Councillor.

I thought, But what about his skin? That's what we've been taught to think. Waste not, want not. Wastefulness is the Action of the Selfish. The Director didn't mention it. The human's largest and most complex organ of all.

During the Great Conflagration, when many people were burned, surgeons couldn't always find enough intact skin on the victim to do grafts. They had to graft it from someone else. Donor skin doesn't grow on the recipient, but it makes a scaffolding for the person's own skin to grow beneath.

We've been learning about it in Conflagration History. We learned how, after some of the big fire-storms, citizens would be queuing up to donate. They got five kilos of flour in exchange.

Mr Winkins's wrinkled dried-fruit face, with his sad wet eyes, swam into my mind. I found myself laughing. That worn-out face would look so funny fitted to a young person.

The laugh turned to a choke. My eyes prickled and emptiness clutched at my stomach. OK, so it was partly afternoon hunger which often makes you feel queasy. But even so, thinking about Mr Winkins was upsetting. Yesterday, he'd been somebody. Now he was nothing. If only I'd bothered to say goodbye properly.

'Seven citizens are to be released from the captivity of their physical incapacity through the generosity of one man. Let us give him our thanks.'

What the Director was saying felt wrong. We were thanking Mr Winkins for body-parts which he didn't need now he was dead. We should've been thanking him for what he'd done in life: the dirty jobs that kept us safe, unblocking drains, cleaning toilets, sweeping out the yard when druggies lobbed their kit over the wall. And he always stood up for the lesser people like Dee.

Callam, next to me, was churned up too. His shoulders heaved. He swallowed tears.

'Long may all lowly and insignificant citizens emulate his example. May Mr Winston's name be honoured forever.'

'Honoured forever.'

Nobody so much as twitched each time the Director got Mr Winkins's name wrong.

As we were filing out of Roll-Call, I overheard our teacher nattering to another. Ms Reed knows gossip's prohibited. It doesn't stop her.

'Shame about Winkins, isn't it? Like losing a limb. A bit of the past.'

'Poor old fellow. Still, at least he was on his own. It's not as though there's anybody going to miss him. And with seven councillors benefiting, it's a blessing in disguise. These simple-minded Low-Castes are a bit like animals. They know when their time's come. They just turn their faces to the wall and stop breathing.'

It wasn't true. Mr Winkins hadn't lived alone. He had a little green budgie. On bright days, he used to put the cage out on his window-ledge. You'd hear it trilling away up there. You aren't supposed to keep pets if you're D-Classified. But the Community Street Wardens never did anything about that bird.

At going-home time, there was something else odd. The notice-board outside, with the school name on it, was covered over with a scrappy bit of paper.

Temporary Change of Use, it said, though it didn't say what sort of change. Then, *Closed till Further Notice. Parents and Pupils Will Await Instructions and Notification.*

It was peculiar.

We three Peddles walked straight home, no deviating through Leicester Square to look at the lights. And definitely no scavvying.

I held Dee's hand tight, and kept Rah's stiff twiggy arm hooked firmly over mine. It began to drizzle on us. It was that sticky kind of rain that leaves greasy smudges.

Something was still making me feel queasy. I hoped I wasn't getting ill. Illness was so disgusting. We used to see some of the sick foreigners just before curfew-time, being pushed out by their attendants, sallow-skinned, pathetic wrecks, gulping from their oxygen flasks. They come to this country for their holidays. But few of them look as though they're enjoying it.

Our Ma Peddle says that in the Pre-Post-War-Zone times there were clinics for people like us where you could go if you were poorly. I wouldn't have liked that. You never know what they might do to you in a clinic. The important thing, I reckon, is never to let yourself get poorly.

'Stinky wrinkly Winkins, he ready steady deady now, in't he?' said Dee cheerfully.

'Yes. Kind Mr Winkins has passed on.' Then I added, because I think it's important for Dee to have a realistic outlook on existence, 'But although it's very sad for us,

29

it's not really so terrible. Everybody turns into a stiff sometime. And you can always remember how he was specially kind to you when the big boys teased you.'

'All people kind,' said Dee smugly, and chanted me one of the Sector songs you get taught in the Infants. 'All Sector workers are kind and good. Treat public carers as you should.'

Rah is not such an optimist. 'Dead, dead,' he kept chanting gloomily. And sometimes, 'Mine.'

'Yes, Rah, Mr Winkins is dead. But no, he isn't yours. He doesn't belong to anyone.'

Though perhaps he did belong to someone? By now, the seven donated parts of him were already functioning away inside seven powerful councillors.

'Stinky Winky got cheepy cheepy,' said Dee.

'What?'

'Cheepy tweety cheeping,' she repeated, louder.

'Dog,' Rah agreed morosely. 'Man-dog. Mine.'

Having conversations with either of them was exhausting. They'd say one word but mean another. You had to work it out for yourself what they really meant. But at least Rah was trying to join in. If he practised, he might get better. Unless, by his age, it's too late to expect improvement.

Our Ma Peddle says he doesn't need improving because he's perfect just as he is. Huh. *She* doesn't have to share a bunk-bed with him.

'Not doggy dog, silly Rah!' said Dee. 'Mr Winkins he got a tweety cheeping *bird*!'

She had a memory for faces, even for budgie bird faces.

I wonder what'll become of it? It's rumoured that unauthorized domestic pets get Speedy Assisted Demise, same as deformed babies.

Getting SAD is supposed to be quick and painfree.

6

Salting the Soup

Such disquiet at school, I forgot our scavvied man.

'He's over there, in the corner,' said Our Ma Peddle. 'Keeping out of the way and minding his own business.'

So she hadn't thrown him out after all. The reverse. She'd made him a cosy rat's bed of straw, rags, and rugs piled on the floor. And she'd hammered a couple of nails into the rafters, tied a bit of rope between them, slung a blanket over.

'So's he's got some privacy from you lot,' she said.

I said, 'Why don't we pull him through to the back room? Then he'd be nice and quiet. Put him on Rah's bed. Rah won't mind, will you?'

'Aaargh man,' said Rah.

'You just leave that fellow where he is! Total rest, that's what he needs, till he's over the worst of it.'

'Don't know why you think he can get any rest in here.'

'I got to keep my eye on him.'

The strip-light overhead glared down on him. We've hitched it up to the street illuminations with a bit of cable out through the window. It has to be on all the time. It didn't bother Our Ma Peddle. But it peeved me. There's old switches on the walls. You used to be able to flick them on and off so you could control the lighting yourself. That was ace.

Shaved and washed, Rah's Man looked younger, not so wild, but still and pale as if he was carved out of a bit of bone.

In the evening, with all of us trooping in, tired and hungry, the kitchen was as scrabbly as a nest of cockroaches. We tried not to quarrel. There just wasn't space for arguments.

31

Rah was flinging his stringy arms about and making deep throaty noises. That's his way of being happy. Dee was trying to teach little Netta to bang a tin mug with a wooden spoon. Netta, gurgling on the floor, liked the attention, though her jerky hands couldn't grip the spoon however vigorously Dee cheered encouragement.

Netta had no control over her body, not even the muscles of her face. She had a lovely lop-sided smile but you had to catch it quick for it only bloomed for a few seconds at a time.

She's new. A neighbour brought her over from the next block, said Our Ma Peddle could have her for 260 R, even though he'd paid 400 R. He might have been lying. He might have picked her out of a skip, then decided she wasn't worth keeping. She's got so many neurological defects. But it was fun having her around.

She was supposed to be a newborn.

'And if she's newborn, then I'm the Queen of Abyssinia,' said Our Ma Peddle. 'Look at all them teeth. Three years if she's a day.'

Netta knew when she was being talked about. She tried to smile. It came out as a grimace.

The noisiest person was our big sister, Pica. She was helping make the soup, crashing about at the stove, slamming down lids, thumping pans. Pica could even peel a potato loudly.

'OUR MA PEDDLE!' she yelled out, as though Ma was over the far side of Trafalgar Square instead of right beside her. 'MUCH?'

Pica speaks in short shouts. She's deaf. Like with Rah and Dee, you have to work out what she's trying to say. Now she meant, How much salt should she add to the cooking pot?

'Just a pinch, Piccadilly. Yes, that'll do.' Our Ma Peddle spoke as though she could see the salt in the

32

palm of Pica's hand. 'We don't want to end up like Dead Sea anchovies, do we? Now, give it a good stir.'

'STIRRING!' Pica roared back.

I said, 'Our Ma, could a person die from deafness?'

'Don't you fret, son. Piccadilly ain't no more like to die of hard of hearing than what I am of not seeing proper. She just got to like it and lump it. And if we love her, we got to lump it too.'

'It's not Pica I'm talking about. It's the school janitor.'

'Old George?'

'Yep. We had special Roll-Call for him. He's passed away. General malaise and deafness.'

Our Ma Peddle's blank milky eyes stared into nothing. Then, brightly, she said, 'Well, fancy that! Poor fellow. Used to work with me, on the water pump. Good team we were. Served the community well.'

'But Our Ma, what's it mean? Did he *really* die of his own accord? Or was he helped?'

'Helped?'

'Speedy Assisted Demise? Like they do with irregular cats and dogs and babies?'

'Now then, Bedford. Don't you think that way. No good'll come of it. That's like spreading false rumour. And you know where that can get you. If he's gone, he's gone. You can't look backwards. Best foot forward, that's the way.'

I said, 'All right. But there's something else, about the man. How did he get cut? Was it a fight?'

'You just mind your own business, son, and pass me the knife.' She slashed away at the peeled vegetables as though our lives depended on it, reducing them to a soft fleshy pulp oozing white juices. How did she manage to chop vegies without nicking off all her fingertips?

The man in the nest began stirring. Pica crashed pans louder. It looked like she was doing it on purpose. She made sheep-eyes at him and smirked. She has such huge dark eyes that the effect was peculiar more than attractive.

'Don't bother, Pica,' I mouthed to her. 'He'll never fancy a sag-bag like you.'

'Bedford! Since you've got time on your hands to taunt your sister, you might as well make a start on the other girls' heads. That'll put a stop to your silly chatter.'

That meant I had to de-louse them. Has to be done every week. Dysfuncs need a lot of looking after. Ma can do most things just by feel. Cutting people's fingernails, hammering nails, first aid, last rites. De-lousing she couldn't.

You need a fine-toothed metal comb and a solution of coal tar soap in a jar. It smells foul.

'Come on, Dee, you first,' I said. She stood patiently beside me and didn't budge even when I tugged, just yelped a bit.

'Ow! Owy! wowy wow! Pully bully bad boy Bee.'

She understood that if it wasn't done, you itched till you nearly went crazy.

'Sorry, Dee,' I said. 'Nearly through.'

You have to be methodical, draw the comb through every single strand of hair, section by section. You mustn't miss a single bug or they do gender recognition and start breeding.

Rah's Man in the corner growled like a scary animal. In the night you hear sounds like that when the drunks and vagrants are being rounded up. The CSW have to keep the streets safe for tourists so they can be taken out to look at the evening light-shows.

7

Nits and Nests

'Our Ma, I think he's in pain.'

'Nonsense,' she snapped through lips tight as a rat-trap. 'Exaggerating. Low pain threshold, that's always the trouble with men. If he got guts enough, he'll pull through.'

She bent down and felt his head. 'Well, maybe he's a bit hot.' But she had nothing to give him apart from the steel-spring of her tongue.

Ma Peddle's strictness is scary if you don't know about her heart of gold. The man swore a bit but eventually he calmed down. Then he pulled aside the blanket curtain and began to stare so intently I felt like a fly watched by a spider.

I unbraided Dee's hair and worked my way through it.

'It is most strange,' the man said with effort. 'Never before do I see small boy coiffeur to small girl. You enjoy to do this?'

'De-lousing time,' I said. 'Got to be done. Looking for nits.'

'What is?'

I thought everybody knew about them. 'Eggs. You have to pick them out before they hatch into lice.'

With all of us living so close, they spread as fast as dengue fever.

According to Our Ma Peddle, in the old days you didn't have to go through such a palaver because there was a potion you could get that killed them once and for all. But she's always going on about the wonderful old days before this was a PWZ. You never know how much of it's true. In our times, medical supplies are for

35

A-Classifieds. And foreign tourists, of course. Otherwise they wouldn't bother to come here, would they? They get loads of things we hardly know about. Those Pineapples Sierra Leone I once saw were for tourists.

'Every day, you must do this?'

'If you can be bothered. But once a week's OK.'

Along the teeth of the comb lay the line of sticky dots I'd dragged from Dee's hair. Before dunking the comb in the soapy water, I showed him. 'If you're really cunning, you catch the bugs too. They're brown. But just combing helps. Breaks their little legs. So they can't hop on to somebody else. They'll just stay with Dee and suck *her* blood, won't they, Dee?'

'Missy messing. Stop it, Bedford,' she said. 'Get on, get on, like a busy bee.'

'I do not care for bed-bugs.'

'No. I told you. Nits. Head-lice eggs.'

For a grown man, he didn't seem to know much.

I finished Dee's head. I replaited it. I tied off each braid with a jolly red bead and bow.

'Thanky danky spanky you, Bedford!' Dee gave me a hurried sort of a kiss before prancing off to do one of her favourite things—telling someone else how to do whatever it was they were already doing. Pica got the stream of advice. Not being able to hear, she ignored it. Dee pointed to the thick brown slurry bubbling in the pot and shouted at Pica that she better keep stirring or it'd burn.

'Yummy!' I said to Pica. 'Don't we all just love the way Pica makes burned soup.'

Even though she probably couldn't hear the words, she guessed the tone. She made dagger eyes at me.

'Set the table, able table. Set it right,' Dee chanted. 'Count the people, count them right. One two, six seven.' Her way of counting was odd, but from time to time the figure she came up with was the right one. It was mostly luck.

Before I could start on little Netta's head, Ma Peddle ordered me to take Rah's Man some water.

The man clasped the mug with both hands. But he was so weak he couldn't hold it steady. I felt sorry for him. I tried to help. But he only wet his lips before pushing the mug away. Poor geezer. He looked rough.

'He must drink it all, Bedford,' Our Ma Peddle said. 'Stand over him while he does.'

'Yes, Ma.'

'Then take him an empty jug. He must use it.'

'What for?'

'You're a man, aren't you? Or d'you fancy carrying him down to the privvy yourself?'

I took the man a tin pot.

'Pull the curtain on him, if you please. He's not the Sector freak-show.'

'Wish he was,' I grumbled. I'd never seen it. Callam has. He said it was side-splitting.

I de-loused Netta's springy thatch of curls. Harder work than handing out piss-pots. Netta protested with jerky spasms.

The man asked, 'So these creatures you are chasing and chastising reside upon the human body like the bed-bug, yet not the bed-bug?'

'Yup,' I said.

'And you now exterminate?'

'Yup.'

'And so they then are parasites? Species who must draw nutrient from other species?'

'Listen,' I said. 'Round here, we got nits and lice, rats and roaches. I don't know about any others. But if you're that worried, maybe you should get your head shaved on a number one? Like Rah and me? See, no hair, no nits, no problem.'

'So why are these girls not shaven also on the head?'

'Because Ma Peddle's soppy. She lets the girls grow

37

theirs if they want. She says it's feminine. Whatever *that* means.'

Our Ma Peddle has ears so sharp I reckon they can hear the snap of a breaking louse-leg. 'My girls,' she interrupted, 'have lost their faculties, their origins, their roots, their first families, their social identities. But that ain't no reason for them to lose their gender definition into the bargain.'

I don't see the point of gender definition if it makes Pica go all silly, swivelling her hips about like a flag just to stir the soup. And if all that wiggling was meant for Rah's Man, he didn't seem to be taking any notice. He was too worried about bugs.

'With so many parasites feeding, life condition are not so good for you.'

I don't care for criticism.

'Listen, pal,' I said. 'You just quit complaining. If it hadn't been for me, you'd be dead and gone by now. Face down in the water and half-way out to the big ocean.' I conveniently omitted that it was Rah who'd found him, not me. 'And even if you hadn't drowned, you'd have been caught by the curfew. They can give you a Caution for that. And Cautions cost. You may not like it with us, but at least you're safe.'

'Safe! Here? You jest.'

'And furthermore,' I went on defensively, 'things are getting better in this Sector every week.'

They told us so in school. 'Sector One in every way, gets better and better day by day.' Even Dee's class had to learn that.

Rah's Man, watching Our Ma Peddle add more water and crusts to the soup, said gravely, 'In my country also, condition once was better. But even now, not so bad as here.'

I think he must have been a sailor. Sailors saw the world. I asked in a whisper so even Our Ma Peddle wouldn't hear, 'Have you ever seen Pineapples Sierra Leone?'

'Pineapple is the fruit. Sierra Leone is the land from which they come.' He'd not only seen them, but tasted one. Their skin was bristled all over like a man's chin, so he said, and sprouting leaves like razors from the top. 'But within, the flesh is sweet and rich. Also prevents scurvy.'

'Bedford! Will you leave that poor man alone and get on with your task!'

'But he's telling me useful things about scurvy.'

Dee squatted on the edge of the rat's nest to play with the man's huge rough toes as though they were counting pegs. He grabbed my arm. 'I am sorry, boy, if I do not show correct thankfulness. It is wrong. You are good people. Please now you will tell me about the girl.'

'Well,' I began, because I thought he meant Dee. 'She's my favourite sister.'

'No. The other one, the young lady.'

'Lady! Pica?' So Pica's gender definition and ogling eyes weren't wasted. 'What d'you want to know?'

'Anything.'

'She's the eldest. She's bossy. She thinks I'm a useless lowly worm. The feeling's mutual.'

'Her name?'

'Piccadilly. Where she was found. In the underground.'

'Under ground? She is a troglodyte?'

'No. It's a transportation metro under the city. People used to hide down there. The Piccadilly line's the dark blue one, runs from Cockfosters somewhere up in the north, then out to the airbase at West Sector Eleven.' I'd never been out as far as Heathrow but I'd seen it marked on the maps.

'Bedford!' Ma Peddle screamed at me across the

kitchen. 'If I told you once, I been telling you a thousand times and some more. Stop pestering.'

'It's not *me* doing the pestering. It's him.'

'Please, ma'am,' Rah's Man defended me. 'Forgive for adding yet more to your work-load. But this boy, he is not at fault and this happy chatter of little children gives me good cheer.'

'MA! BEDFORD! SOUP'S UP!' Pica yelled. I fetched the mugs to fill. Potato and yam, flavoured with fish-bones, thickened with bread.

When I took Rah's Man his share, Pica watched me like a jealous cat. I said to him, 'Do you a deal, pal. You tell me yesterday's Tale-Times, what happened to Joseph in the pit. I tell you about Pica.'

Perhaps I shouldn't have. For if I hadn't, he might not have fallen for her, and she'd still be here treating me like a lowly worm.

Strange how much I miss her roaring voice.

8

Tequila Sunrise

He watched Pica as she crashed about like a deaf elephant.

'So truthfully this is your real sister?'

'Not flesh and blood. But very real, worst luck.'

'Also tall boy, is such a real brother?'

''Course. Rah just looks that way, because, well because that's the way he is. His brain wasn't structured properly.'

'And the mother, who is so old, like grandparent?'

I'd never thought of Our Ma Peddle having any age. She just was.

'If that is mother, where is father?'

'Don't need one. Men are a waste of space.' That was one of Our Ma Peddle's sayings. 'Now, shall I continue with the story of the oh-so-lovely Piccadilly?'

'Please.'

'Well, she's classified MIQ. That's medium range, much too bright to work in the SWU with Rah. She's chambermaid in the Royal Elizabethan Hotel, over on Shaftesbury Avenue. Our community council makes sure that every citizen has a useful function.'

The mission statement's written up on the school walls to remind us. *City Sector One, the caring Sector. A place for everybody. Everybody in their rightful place. The child's place is in his school.*

'Pica started in a West Sector Eleven hotel, out near the airbase. But then got moved back here. Our Ma Peddle was really glad. She says you don't know what happens to girls in Sector Eleven.'

'Is your sister so angry?'

'No. Just deaf as a blinking post. And stubborn as a

41

mule. She was caught in one of the big raids. Afterwards, nobody came and claimed her. So Ma Peddle brought her home.'

If you were anywhere near a Big Albert, so Ma said and she was a fire-fighter so she should know, it blew your eardrums right out.

'So she was lucky not to be killed?'

'Lucky? You joking? Pica really suffered. You should've *heard* how she used to scream. Some nights we even got Cautions from the Wardens about it. Tourists don't like screaming. They can't enjoy their holidays properly.'

She still did scream, but only in her sleep. Ma Peddle and the two little girls had to put up with it, just like I had to put up with Rah's wetting. That's called Family Life, putting up with one another, liking it and lumping it.

Rah's Man kept to his side of the deal and told me what I'd missed from Tale-Times, how Joseph got rescued from the pit and journeyed to a distant land. Then he told me what was going to happen in the next bit.

'There will be terrible famine. Joseph become rich, wise ruler. He take care of elder brothers, like you take care of sisters.'

I liked that bit, being good to someone, even if they've been rotten to you. I said, 'How come you know the ending of Ma's story when she hasn't told it yet? Have you got future vision?'

'Joseph story is known in my land also.'

'You sure?' I thought Our Ma Peddle made up Tale-Times as she went along.

'No, it is not make-believe. It is true tales from the book of the Mother Church. This holds poetry and beliefs and true histories of past conflicts, scourges, disasters.'

42

I said, 'Low-Castes aren't allowed books at home. They'd put the wrong kind of ideas into our minds. Then we wouldn't be able to do the jobs they need us to do.'

Callam's allowed books at home. But he's not Low-Caste. He's from a proper TATCH family with two adults, two children. If you're TATCH you're allowed books, and domestic indoor pets, and television, and skilled jobs. Callam's dad works for UNOC and his mum's a driver. They've been allocated an apartment in one of the new Residencies. I've never seen inside but Callam's told me.

Even though Callam's an A-Classified High-Caste TATCH he still likes being my friend.

There was more roaring in the night. It wasn't Pica or Rah and it wasn't the stray dogs outside. It was Rah's Man.

'Vatn, Vatn,' he kept shouting. I reckoned that Pica definitely overdid the salt in that soup. That's just the sort of daft thing she does when she burns the food, puts in lots of something else to hide the cindery taste. Sometimes vinegar. Sometimes pepper. This time salt.

When the fifth bout of raging disturbed me, I went through to see what was up. Rah's Man croaked out from behind the blanket screen, 'Vatn.'

It was easy to guess what he wanted. I fetched him the pitcher but it was difficult for him to drink lying down. He raised the mug to his mouth awkwardly. So much precious water that I'd lugged up four flights of steps dribbled down his neck. But he gulped on like he was filling a sand-hole in a desert.

Then he flung his covering of rags and newspapers aside. He was so hot I could feel it radiating off him like a furnace.

'D'you want the piss-pot?' I whispered.

He did.

When I took away the full jug, I knew he must be very ill. I reckoned he'd be dead by morning. His pee was streaky pink. Fantastic. Just like a fancy cocktail.

At the Royal Elizabethan the bartender mixes up primo multi-coloured concoctions for the guests. You can see him through the big windows pouring different coloured liqueurs into a cocktail glass before putting the tiny paper parasol on top.

'Look! You've made yourself a Tequila Sunrise!' I said. Just because he was dying seemed no reason not to try and give him one last laugh.

He nodded but didn't smile.

'You all right, mate?' I asked, which was pretty stupid under the circumstances.

'It is all fine and excellent. You are good people.'

'You want anything else? Cold cloth on your head? Hot brick for your feet?'

'The old mother says to drink with frequency, maintain function of remaining organ. One kidney now for two must labour.'

'You only got one kidney?' I was beginning to understand what the wound in his side was about. What a moron I was not to have realized before.

With the bedding thrown off, I could see the scar, red and inflamed, as bright as a Bloody Mår̥y in the Rainbow Lounge bar of the Royal Elizabethan. Crisscrossed with different coloured threads where Our Ma Peddle had sewn him up. Typical of her darning. That's how she mends our socks. Rough and ready and can't see the colours.

'Someone cut out a kidney before you're even dead? So you're a living donor!'

'It is long known,' he said wearily, 'that the live

44

transplantation of any organ must always be more satisfactory for the recipient than when taken from the already deceased.'

I was angry. 'You sold it, didn't you? You're disgusting! Worse than filth. I hate creeps like you. I wish we'd never brought you here!' I couldn't stop myself kicking him hard. Only afterwards did I consider that courteous Joseph who became an Egyptian ruler wouldn't have done that.

But the man was an addict. He must be. That's the only reason why somebody has one of their organs removed while they're still alive. They swap it for the drugs they want. Druggies'll sell anything, even the hair off their heads to wig-makers. And when they haven't anything left to sell, they'll nick something off someone else. Your ration tokens, your ID, your shoes. They were worse than drunks. At least the drunks who clustered like maggots down the bottom of Villiers Street only frightened you by shouting and lurching about.

'No!' he said. 'I did not sell. This part was stolen by thieves in clean uniform. I am not a fool. I am victim.'

I didn't believe a word of it. 'You're lying through your teeth!' I said.

'When I am well, I prove to you the sincerity of my gratitude. I shall do all I can to help you get away.'

'Away? I don't want to get away. I'm fine here. This is my home. Peddle's Palace.'

'Not only you. Also these others you call your family. This is a wicked city, even if there yet are some good folks. But it is not safe. You must get out before this same disaster occurs to you that has befallen me.'

I said, 'Why don't you just belt up and go to sleep?' I gave him another kick, not quite so hard, and I crept back to my room feeling nauseated.

'Poor bloke,' I muttered as I climbed on to the upper bunk. The lower one stank as bad as a condemned hospice.

By morning, his fever was down. He was sitting up, then standing. He could walk at geriatric's pace across the kitchen to take a place on the wooden bench. Pica sidled in beside him. They sat close. He didn't speak, only took her hand and held it on his lap. She sat, pop-eyed as a startled bluebottle, and gazed into his bone-white face.

Gender definition, yuck. Happy as a pair of head-lice.

Later, when Our Ma Peddle was behind the curtain dressing his wound, he seemed to be arguing with her.

'And you're just a foreign denizen,' I heard her hiss. 'You don't know nothing. Just because we look like a PWZ. But there's rebuilding planned. We'll be great again. You'll see.'

When I went down to fetch water from the standpipe, he followed me all the way. In spite of the zazzy darning in his side, he insisted on helping me carry one of the buckets.

'The old woman doesn't understand. But you do.'

'Understand what?'

'The situation. Why you have here so many visitors?'

'Tourists,' I said. 'It's no secret. Historic tourism. *Main trade. Good trade. Great trade.* Everybody knows. They fly in from all over. *Enjoy the Sights of Olde Englande With The Kindest of Care.*'

We knew the slogans inside out. Holiday breaks were good trade.

Rah's Man slammed down the bucket so that valuable water slopped out. He grabbed my shoulder and made me look at him. The whites of his eyes were yellow.

'Little boy,' he said, 'why would any world citizen who is not crazy, *pazzo, fou, folle*, take recreation in PWZ?'

'I told you. Because it's the ideal city for the four-day break.'

'You have spoken sometime to tourists?'

I shook my head.

'Not permitted. "LC citizens are prohibited from endeavouring to seek fraternity with, or in any other way causing irritation to, esteemed visitors." That's part of Community Living Regulation 128A.'

'And why do these so many, so wealthy, ersatz tourists arrive in wheeling chairs with cylinders of breathing oxygen attached to foot-rest? Why supported by nursing attendants? Why leave walking, rosy-face, and so well?'

'I dunno.' I trawled my brain for an appropriate mission statement that we all knew. ' "Tourists first because tourists matter. Tourists are our bread and butter." '

'Not tourists. Visitors come here to be made well. To receive new parts.'

'That's good then,' I said. 'If sick people get better you should be the first person to be pleased because that's just what Ma Peddle's done for you.'

'The old woman repaired me, yes. But she did not rob and plunder from another to achieve her act of mercy.'

9

How Many Beans Make Five?

Night curfew ends at seven with a siren. Shortly after, the street tannoys began blaring out, ordering all young citizens of City Sector One to report to their school or Special Work Unit.

Rah was bleating like a goat all the way, and Dee jumping up and down with excitement.

'What happen? What going going gone?'

'I don't *know*, Dee. I told you. I haven't a clue.'

During our school's 'Temporary Change of Usage' it had become the Sector's temporary IYSRAC centre, whatever that was. There was a new notice taped over the previous note on the board outside.

We were let in through the heavily fortified main gate by a Community Health and Welfare Monitor in her neat white uniform. That was odd. CHAWMs didn't usually come into school any more than CSWs did. But she was pleasant and smiling and greeted each of us by our name instead of by our ID code. She keyed each person off on her memory pad.

I enquired, most politely, because of it being an offence to approach any community worker in an uncouth manner, 'Excuse me, but please, Miss, what's all this IYSRAC stuff?'

'It's the temporary redesignation, dear,' she said. She had light blue eyes and a nice fresh smell. Most people don't smell so good if you get too close.

'Yeah, Miss, but what's it mean?'

'IYSRAC, dear? They've already informed you. It's the Infant and Youth Special Re-Assessment Centre.'

That word 'special' I should've watched out for. Anything special's bound to start smelling bad before long. Mr Winkins had been driven to a Special Medi-Care Unit when he was picked up. Rah's workplace is called special too.

I hate the way Rah and the other low-grade Abs get made to do that dreary work. The only special thing about the SWU is that it's specially boring.

But Ma Peddle says, compared to how Dysfuncs and Abs used to be treated, it's not such a bad system. In those times, most of them got a Speedily Assisted Demise with a long needle straight into the chambers of the heart before they were even born.

We were all pleased to be back at school, to see our friends, even if it wasn't called a school any more. Dee darted off to join a boisterous game of hopscotch. For a DJLDS she's quite agile. I led Rah to the SWU entrance.

Surprise! The bleating goat was quite content to be back. One of the other Abs, a stunted lad with a bulging head as abnormally large as Rah's was small, welcomed him as heartily as some long-lost uncle.

'Yearrgh, 'lo 'lo 'lo, Rah, my man!' the misshapen gnome cackled.

Rah wrapped his arms round his workmate's neck. They then sat down at the workbench to wait for their Overseer to bring them the boxes of nuts and bolts that needed sorting.

The Overseer was an Ab too, a microcephalic. He took his job seriously. Classifying tiny parts from defused landmines may not be everybody's idea of important work. But it wasn't such a lousy occupation if it meant Rah could be with companions, usefully serving our community in one of the few ways they were able. The Sector Mission Statement says there's a place for everyone. Maybe it's right and this workshop really is the right place for Rah.

As I left the Unit, Rah flashed me a happy monkey smile.

'Bye, Rah!' I waved. 'Have a good day. See you later. Same time?'

'Yeergh.'

'Same place?'

'Yeergh.'

It has to be the same time and place. Rah couldn't find his own way down a straight line even if it was chalked on the road in front of him.

At first, it felt like it was going to be a normal morning, except that we weren't made to tax our brains with Logarithms and World History. We mucked about in the yard instead. Someone got hold of an inner tube to kick about. There was a cheerful atmosphere. Nobody likes being stuck at home all the time. Even Middle-Castes and Upper-Castes like Callam who've got nice apartments with lifts and running water, get fed up not seeing their mates. Ma Peddle says she thinks extra curfews are worse for people like them than for people like us.

I said, 'At least they can watch cartoons on their televisions.'

She said, 'Watch stupidvision more like.'

I shouldn't have expected her to envy something that involves looking with your eyes.

She said, '*And* they don't have Tale-Times, do they? So which would you prefer, Bedford? Same stale cartoon all day, or an hour of Tale-Times?' I didn't know then that she didn't make up all her stories but that she'd got them out of that book Rah's Man was on about.

Eventually we were filed up to our classrooms. And after we'd saluted the Sector flag, another of the Community and Health Welfare Monitors came in. She had a really sweet smile and little wisps of blonde hair curling out from under her white cap. Her white shoes were spotless. CHAW Monitors manage to keep so clean, even when they're out on the streets seeing to old drunks in the gutter.

'Today, dear children,' she told us, 'your teachers have been granted a well-earned day-break. And you will be having your repeat medicals.'

A groan went round the class. There's medicals every trimester. They weigh you, look for nits, measure your height against the metre-stick, test your teeth for rot, check your radiation levels.

They never find anything interesting. It's just something that gets you off Logarithms.

'*Repeat* medicals?' said Callam who sat next to me when this was our school, and who's still sitting next to me now it's an IYSRAC.

Politely, he raised his hand. 'Excuse me, but what for?'

'Nothing to be alarmed about, dear,' the CHAW Monitor said with her sunny smile. 'Entirely routine. As you very well know, a healthy community is a strong community.'

'Preventative care saves wear and tear,' I added without thinking. If I *had* been thinking, I'd have known that that was the moment to blunder out of the classroom, go along to Dee's, grab hold of her, and run and run as far as we could until our legs dropped off. But I didn't think of it at the time.

10

Keeping Tabs on You

Down in the hall, they had us sitting cross-legged on the floor in tidy lines. Each person had to go behind the white screens at the far end, undress, and be examined.

It was very boring, waiting. The day ticked on. These medicals were taking longer than usual. At first, they just seemed to be sorting out mainstreamers and A-Classifieds from Abs, Dysfuncs, and LCs. But then it seemed to be more complicated than that. By the afternoon a lot of pupils had been sent home. This was good. The hall was less crowded. You could stretch your legs out. It seemed like the rest of us were going to be tested all over again.

I caught sight of Dee. Still here. The only one left from her class. I was glad. I didn't want her being sent home before me. She was being so good, sitting quite still, droopy mouth moist and her big pink tongue just peeking out, arms neatly folded, slanty eyes ahead. Ma Peddle has trained her to be socially acceptable in any situation.

Of course there's no way she could ever be classified as anything other than DJLDS. When you're trisomic, every cell of your body is affected.

'What's going on?' a voice behind whispered anxiously. It was A-Classified, HC, HIQ, TATCH child Callam. He's never a Dysfunc. So what's he doing still here?

I shrugged. 'Haven't a clue, chum. But it's nothing for you to worry your busy little brain-cells about.'

'D'you think they're checking out all the Dysfuncs?'

''Course they are, you chump. Any fool can work that one out.'

Callam said, 'So why are *you* still here? Everybody knows about all your dopey family. But *you're* not like the rest of them, are you?'

'I'm Low-Caste, aren't I?'

'Are you really? I've never really thought about it.'

I thought, You wouldn't, if you weren't. I said, 'Because of no parents. I was a street foundling.'

Our Ma Peddle had told me exactly where she found me. In a narrow alley called Bedford Court off Bedfordsbury. I've been to check it out loads of times. It's good to know where your life began.

'Oh. Sorry.'

'No need to be. My folks are fine.'

Callam was trembling, like Rah does before he takes one of his seizures. But in Callam's case it looked like the quakes of fear. I tried to reassure him. 'Listen, Callam. You know you're not LC. It's bound to be an admin mistake. They'll soon find out.'

'No mistake. I'm an Ab.'

Now it was my turn to be surprised. How could he be? He didn't bleat or wave his arms about like Rah. He hadn't got distinguishing characteristics or forty-seven chromosomes like Dee. He wasn't a CP like Netta. I said, 'Well you don't look it.'

'That's because I'm not some weird mental defective,' he said angrily. 'I haven't got any intellectual abnormalities. It's just a small physical impurity.' He pulled off his boot, pulled back his sock, and for a brief second, I saw his foot. Short and stumpy, only half the length of the boot. At the end were six toes, the two big ones fused together at the base, but with two toenails.

'Wow,' I said. 'Just look at that! How come?'

'Dunno. Born that way.' He pulled up the sock, laced up the boot.

'Didn't your mum want to do something about it?' I said.

53

Stupid! There wasn't much a mother could do about a defective baby. Dump it in a skip? Advertise it for private sale?

'I hate it. Don't tell anyone, will you?'

''Course not. Cross my heart.'

'No one knows, apart from Mum and Dad. Not even my sister. What d'you think they're going to do to me? See, I've never had the full medical before. I've always got off.'

'I shouldn't worry. You TATCH kids are all in the fast lane. They'll probably just make a note of it on your records.'

I felt sorry for him. His attitude. His shame. At least no one in my family's ashamed of dysfunctions.

Once, when I was younger, I asked Dee if she would've preferred to have been born without her extra chromosome so she'd be like all the other little girls.

What in heck made me think she wanted to be other people?

'Nobody the same. This me. That you. Every little busy body somebody different,' she told me firmly.

'But don't you sometimes wish,' I persisted, 'that you'd got a really good brain like mine?'

'No no nopey ropey nope.'

'Or a proper face?'

'Nope.'

'Or a proper nose, not a funny little button in the middle?'

'Nope.' She was beginning to giggle. She crinkled up her slanty eyes. 'You silly-billy Bedford boy. I me. I like me. I Dee Peddle.'

Such serenity in her identity. And there's sad clever Callam frightened about his own toes.

When it was his turn to be called, he went as pale as potato soup. As he walked towards the screen, I noticed for the first time the slight drag of his six-toe foot, how he had to lift it with every step.

Fingers crossed. 'You'll be all right,' I whispered after him.

Finally, it was my turn again. These examinations were very thorough. ECGs, blood tests, urine tests, liver function tests, sight scans. Every detail tapped into the keypad. The doctor was really nice.

'Thank you for your patience and co-operation,' she said. She shook my hand, gave me a brown sealed envelope to take home to my parent or carer and told me I could go. But Dee was still in there. Callam too. So I waited on the stairs till they were through with them as well.

I reckoned that since Our Ma Peddle was only a surrogate parent, and sightless with it so that she'd be asking me to read the letter aloud to her later on anyway, I might as well open it now.

It was some kind of consent form with boxes to fill in. It explained that, as part of the new health plan, certain carefully selected individuals were to return to IYSRAC tomorrow when their tagging would commence.

I went back into the hall. One of the junior CHAWMs was putting away the equipment. I asked her what it all meant.

'Just a safety measure, dear. So we can keep an eye on our vulnerable little ones when they're out and about.'

I said, 'But the CS Wardens do that.'

'They can't keep an eye on health levels. They're not, well, you know, trained for that type of supervision, not like we are.' I reckon she didn't really think wardens were up to it, in the brain department.

'What's tagging mean?'

'It's ever so clever. A teeny-weeny electronic implant. It saves them having to carry their IDs and the HAB can check on people's well-being right round the clock.

A really sensible precaution for citizens who are poorly. It means we can prioritize healthcare resources.'

'*I'm* not poorly. I've never been poorly.'

'Then it won't bother you, will it, dear?' She gave me a glowing smile and a pat on the head.

Callam wasn't poorly either. He just had one toe too many. But he was crying when he walked across the yard clutching his unopened brown envelope.

'Chin up, Callam!' I shouted. 'Best foot forward.'

We'd done a lot together, him and me. Fighting and making up, ever since our first day in Infant class.

Over in SWU they'd been having medicals too. Rah can't have minded because when Dee and I went to pick him up he was chirpy as a flea. It was only as we were walking home that he began trailing slowly. We kept having to stop and wait for him to catch up. By the time we got to the crossing at Shaftesbury Avenue, he was lagging so far behind I had to go back and pull him along by the hand. Sometimes his meandering snail's pace really irritated me. He was a burden on everything I ever did. It was like having to drag a great sack around with you.

'What's up then, Rah?' I said, more nicely than I felt.

He looked down with his I'm-a-mystified-dog expression.

'Eggy peggy leggy!' said Dee, trying to help.

'I can see perfectly well it's his leg,' I snapped.

'Hurting Rah,' said Dee.

I made him sit down on the pavement. I pulled off his boot. I checked inside. Rah was so dim that even if he had something sharp, like a bit of gravel, inside his boot, it didn't occur to him to do anything about it. One time Ma Peddle found he'd been limping around with a wooden clothes-peg tucked into the heel of his sock.

I turned his boot upside down and shook. Nothing fell

out. As I lifted up his foot to replace his boot, he winced.

'What?'

'Ow,' he said and gestured towards the sky.

'No, Rah. It doesn't hurt you up in the sky,' I said as patiently as I could. 'You have to show me *where* it hurts on *you*.'

He grinned broadly at me so all his crooked teeth showed. He does that when he wants to be helpful. Our Ma Peddle's been training him to understand that roaring when you're in difficulty doesn't help, whereas keeping calm does. So Rah's new idea of being co-operative is to grin like an ape.

I laced up his boot. He winced again. I saw what was hurting him. On his skinny leg, just above the ankle bone, there was a small rectangular strip of something shiny, neatly seated in the flesh.

Rah had been tagged.

It was plastic-coated metal with black and white bar-code lines, and the figures 0 5 1112042 2. That was his number. Everything you might need to know about him was right there. So even at that moment, someone somewhere knew who he was, where he was, and how he was, could monitor the pumping of his heart, the flexing of his flaccid muscles, the level of his red blood corpuscles, the blinking of his eyes, the fluctuation of his brain activity (if any). The only thing they couldn't know was what he was thinking. But being Rah, he didn't do much thinking anyway.

'Me,' he nodded at the strip. 'Rah. Mine.' He seemed both perplexed and pleased, like a trainee CSW might be pleased with his new tattoo. Then he began to pick at the edges as though it was a favourite scab ready to come off.

'Leave it alone, Rah,' I said. 'There's a good man. You'll only make it more sore if you keep touching it.'

There was no obvious sign of damage, though they must have made an incision. Perhaps it was no worse than having ear-studs or nose-rings done.

'Mine,' he insisted. 'Mine.'

'That's right, my old fruit,' I agreed. I took his hand and held it gently till we were home. Given what happened eventually, I'm glad about that, that there's a few worthy memories left.

11

The Ankle Bone

Rah's Man wasn't Rah's any more. Before our eyes he'd been turning into Pica's Man. He stuck to her like he was her tourist attendant, walked her down to the Royal Elizabethan for her first shift of the day, then was back there to meet her and walk her home. He massaged her tired chambermaid's feet with cooking lard. He listened to her raucous voice with a daft gaze of affection.

But when he found out about that little electronic bug just above Rah's ankle bone, he abandoned Pica and went bounding across the kitchen, crashing into Dee, leaping over Netta, and fizzling with fury like he was a stick of dynamite. His yellow jaundiced eyes glowed dangerously.

'How dare, how dare?' he spat. 'Deface beauty and innocence! This dear unsullied spirit.'

When Rah's peed himself in the night, he doesn't strike me as an unsullied spirit. But each to his own vision.

He spoke softly to Rah, stroking his shoulder, coaxing him to stretch his leg out. He slipped from his pocket a small gadget. It was that red-handled knife he'd had on him when we found him. He opened it so that all the hidden tools spread into a glinting steel fan—razor, tooth-saw, pry-bar, clippers, spear knife, wrench, syringe. A total life-protection kit packed into the size of a strong man's thumb. He saw my admiration.

'Olden times Swiss Army knife,' he grunted.

'I know.'

'Was the best. Still now the best. Knife always better than bomb.'

He flicked through the tiny blades, selecting the one to use. Pica, Dee, and I closed in to watch.

'YOU'RE LIKE THE DOCTOR MAN!' Pica roared her good-natured approval. 'DOCTOR! DOCTOR!' She liked a joke.

'Cut him, yeah, cut him! Here come chopper man chop off his head! Chip chop!' sang Dee. I put my hand over her mouth to shut her up.

'This will pain you, Rah,' the man said as he held Rah's leg firmly. He was keeping the probe well out of Rah's sight. 'But more pain for you now, so fewer pain for future.'

Rah, relaxed and trusting, grinned his co-operative grin, all teeth bared. He couldn't know what was about to happen. He was enjoying being the centre of attention.

'Mine. Man,' he said, leaning forward to point to the implanted tag. Man pushed his hand out of the way and Rah didn't even flinch when Man first started prodding.

Bad timing? Bad luck, or what? Ma Peddle came in at the moment when Rah's happy ape-smile gave way to a piercing howl. It was the terrible cry like when a dog's leg is caught in a clawed trap. Man finished prising out the tag as quickly as he could, and dropped it with a clink on the table. It clicked faintly like a shiny beetle on its back.

Ma Peddle couldn't follow what was going on. She knew only that somebody was hurting one of her precious treasures. I tried to hold her back, explaining about the medicals, the sealed letters. It wasn't easy with Dee rabbiting her own version of events which included a lot of unnecessary detail about the number and sharpness of blades on the Swiss self-defence weapon which only made Ma Peddle more angry.

'Who d'you think you are, you audacious beggar? To interfere with my children's well-being behind my back?

What a fine way to show gratitude. If the Sector's numbered him, that'll be for his benefit, bless his little heart. Our Sector cares for us from cradle to grave.'

'Ma'am, if you believe this, you surely are living in cuckoos cloud land. So, if you please, you must take advice. Leave when you can. Take these young people to safety.'

'We don't need none of your intrusion to tell us where we're safe. They'll be moving us into new accommodation just as soon as they can get it ready. I'll have you know, I was a fire-fighter in my time. They don't forget us. I got me medal for that.'

'Your authorities will cherish you because once you were courageous? Because they give out tin discs on ribbon, you think they care? The truth is, no they will not. That all is fairy-tales. There is more truth in the tales you are telling in the evening. And the blindness in your heart is greater than the blindness in your eyes.'

Man was getting up steam. Pica, unable to follow with her ears, was following with her eyes.

'So how you accept such condition? Such much filth you must live with! When rain, you are flood. Window unrepair. Outside, too much water. Inside, no water. In my land poorest family have water within his house. Here the young boy must walk out with the bucket like nomad in the desert.'

Ma Peddle never took criticism. She became defensive. 'Don't go thinking I haven't heard you whispering to my boy, feeding him all sorts of lies what ain't true. Trying to turn him against me and his community. Considering the situation what they been up against, they been doing a pretty grand job. Been providing us with more than adequate. Ration coupons we get, every week, without fail.'

'For what exchange? For pig food! Yams and black potatoes!'

'Don't go on at me, young man, because all of a sudden I got myself a pair of cloth ears and I ain't listening to no more.' Ma Peddle stomped over to the sink and began thrashing about with the vegetable knife.

Man was sweating with frustration. He went on trying to make her listen. 'Ma'am, I accept your succour. But for the sake of your Piccadilly, I cannot accept idealism also. You are danger. Theft to my person can occur next time to one of these children.'

'So you was unlucky. Or acted stupid more like, hanging around after curfew with vagrants and hooligans. Chance in a million what happened to you.'

'Since you do not know it, I must tell. This your city is organ transplant centre. This now is one trade to flourish. Your agriculture? It fail. Livestock? It disease. Automobile industry, armaments industry, all finish. Medical expertise. Yes, A1. Donor transplants. But donation, this means freely to give. Not to pluck from the vulnerable.'

'Now you've gone too far. You hold your tongue, young man!' Ma screamed back. 'Terrifying my little chicks out of their wits to make yourself seem so clever. I treated you like a son. But you been more like some festering albatross hanging round my neck.'

When she gets her knife into you, she really twists it.

'You don't have nothing decent to your name, not even self-respect as what I can see.'

She flailed about with her sturdy red hands trying to grab him. If she'd got hold of him, I reckon she'd have stabbed him with the knife.

'I'm going down to get water,' I said quietly to Man. 'You going to lend a hand?'

He took the tag off the table and followed me. He chucked the tag into a skip. Anybody tracking it would have to dig through layers of rubbish before they found it, and even then, they wouldn't find Rah attached to it any more.

Half-way upstairs with the water, Man stopped and pulled out that scrap of card he'd had on him when we found him.

'You can read?' he asked.

' 'Course I can. We're not savages.'

'Then for you to see.' He handed me the card very carefully, as though afraid I might drop it. I didn't tell him I'd seen it before, though this time I guessed that the lines were supposed to be some sort of a map. But I still couldn't understand the writing.

'*Kreutz*,' he said.

'Yeah, OK. But what's it mean?'

'*Croix*. First you find crossway, then sanctuary for unhoused persons.' He took the card back from me and put it away. 'So you must endeavour soon to alter Old Peddle in her mind. And if you are not succeed, you yourself must find priest of the cross within the charnel house and by this route you flee.'

'You mean run away? Escape? Leaving my family behind? Oh no, I'd never go without the rest of them.'

I'd thought about the Tale-Times man who made the wooden ark to get away from the doom. He took his people with him.

I said, 'I couldn't go without my Ma. She needs me. I have to help her with the younger ones, don't I?'

It wasn't Ma Peddle so much as Dee that I could never leave.

That night there were scufflings and scrabblings through the wall. In our Sector you hear loads of strange sounds. Sirens and screams, yowls and howls. You learn to blank them out. If you worried about every single noise, you'd go barmy. That's where Pica's lucky. What she can't hear doesn't upset her.

63

I suppose I only understood the half of it. The sounds I heard were Pica and her man packing up.

In the morning, the rat's nest was empty. Pica's Man had gone. Pica too. She'd taken her blanket, her spoon, and her tin mug. I guess that means she isn't planning on coming back.

12

Mother Love

'No surprises there,' said Ma Peddle with a grim look.

'But without saying goodbye!' I said. 'I bet he forced her! All that high-falutin talk about not stealing living human bits from each other. And now he's stolen my whole sister.'

Without Pica, it was quiet. No shouting, crashing, or charcoal soup to look forward to. There was a gap in the stuffy air where she used to be. But Ma Peddle was all matter-of-fact, like that time I told her about Mr Winkins. She carried on as though nothing had changed. 'We'll all meet up again one day, won't we, ducks? Beyond the Great Divide, cradled in the breast of the Mother Church, in the Great Hereafter.'

'But aren't you even a tiny bit bothered about Pica now?'

'She's old enough to make up her own mind where she wants to be, who she wants to be with. You'll understand it when you're older. Ready to leave, she was. Needs to make her own family now. Hormones playing up. And it'll start happening to you too, you'll see. All of a sudden, you'll want to be away and making your own life.'

I guessed she was on about gender definition again. Yuk. I hate that kind of talk.

But she was right that Pica hadn't been lured away. There was a scribbly note for Ma left by the stove. I read it out.

Deer deer deerest MA. You will always know you are Best Ever, Kindest. I culd not have wanted for more or beter. I'm away now to take my chanss with Peder.

When we are setlled, I trie lett you knew. Plese kis
Netta from me. I mis her mor thin I cay say. One day
I get my own babbies. Take care MA. Yours, ever,
sign, Piccadilly Peddle. (4590BN7887PLS260/P)

So was there a special kiss for me? No way. No
message, no kiss, no nothing. Huh. Good riddance to
them both. I hated them for not taking me with them.
They didn't even offer me the chance.

Ma Peddle knew I was down. She had the second
sight that way. Without seeing your long face, she knew
how you felt inside. She came and sat on the bench
beside me.

'You won't go brooding over what that fellow said,
Bedford love, will you? 'Course I know about them
transplantations. Nothing new. They been doing them
darn things long before any Great Conflagration. And a
great benefit to mankind too. I wouldn't say no to a
couple of new peepers myself. And a nice new ticker for
Dee. I'm proud of our Sector for what it done for the
sick. But we ain't none of us surgeons so there ain't no
sense in meddling in medical things what don't concern
us.

'By the way, pet,' she said, drawing me closer to her.
'I got a little something for you. Been saving it, for a
special occasion.' She put her hand into her apron
pocket where she kept clothes pegs, little bits of string,
odd socks, and she pulled out two hard brown nuts.

She crushed them together in her strong hands till the
shells cracked. 'Walnuts,' she said, giving me the
kernels.

'Thanks Ma.' They had a funny bitter taste. I wasn't
sure I liked it. But since she'd saved them specially for
me, they must be all right.

'We used to have loads of them in the old days,
specially at Gift-Time.'

Gift-Time was their winter feasting week. Everybody used to join in, Dysfuncs, Abs, CS Wardens, councillors, A-Classifieds, right down to Low-Castes, all handing oranges and nuts to one another, or so Ma said. It was hard to imagine people wanting to give away their foodstuffs, specially not to Wardens. Mostly you just want to keep out of their way.

'That's just what it was all about, Bedford. A celebration. Giving and not counting the cost. I told you the story of the first Gift-Time. The king from afar what brought the gift of gold to the infant king. Don't you never hang on to nothing what I tell you?'

Yes, of course I remembered it, just as I remembered the lion with the thorn in his paw, and the goblets in the sack of corn, and the gold spun from straw.

'But there's so many stories, Ma. How can you keep them separate in your head?'

'It don't really matter if you can't. You find you get to remember them just as they should be when you need them.' She wrapped her arms round me in a strong bear-hug. 'You know what, Bedford, I'm going to be relying on you from now on. My right-hand man, that's you.'

Pressed close to her, I could smell the grease in her long hair. It was familiar and secure.

'We'll be all right, lad, don't you worry. So long as we stick together. That's what families is for.'

I have to believe her, have to love her. There isn't anyone else. My re-cycled family, that's all I have. We don't even have Gift-Times any more.

As she unwrapped her arms from me, I noticed the white dots like grains of rice sticking in her hair.

Lose a sister. Gain a whole new generation of head-lice. Tomorrow I'll have to see to it for her.

Next day, the neat red rectangle of Rah's tag wound was weeping with infection.

'If only that man had left well alone, this wouldn't never have happened,' Ma said.

Why blame it on him?

13

Water Games

I told Dee we weren't going back to school.

'Why why why? Got my lesson. Gotta do learn-to-read.' She knew reading was important. Rah couldn't read. He was a dingbat. Dee could so nearly read.

'*I'll* teach you,' I said. 'When we're not busy. You're a big girl now. You have to help Ma look after Netta, just like Pica used to.'

She's always on about wanting to be useful. Here's her chance.

'See, it's dangerous if you go where I can't see you. There's bad people who might want to take something which you need to keep for yourself.'

'Aaah,' she said. 'Something new. Something blue. Who got something nice for you.' Did she understand?

'It's inside you.'

'Yummy nummy food.'

'Not food. Important parts. But they can't get them if we don't let them.'

'Maybe cry-baby-bunting inside?'

Our Ma had taught us about the reproductive sciences, a confusing lesson since we knew perfectly well that none of us had emerged from her womb in the sticky way she described.

'No, Dee, it's not babies. It's organs they want. They stole Man's kidney to use for somebody else. We don't want them to do that to you or me. We must protect ourselves.'

'Yeeargh! They rip him open!' she said, adding her own gory detail. 'With fork! Then spoon. And spike!' Was she remembering the removal of Rah's tag? 'Them wicked girls. You got it too, Bedford, them itty-bitty bits?'

'Yup. We all got them.'

'How you know?'

'Because I'm a whole can of fish smarter than you and I'm stronger than you. We got to stick close. I'll protect you. But right now, you be a good girl and help Ma while Rah and I go for the water.'

I wasn't to know they'd find Rah anyway, even without his tag.

I don't like cheating on Our Ma. But sometimes you have to. When Dee handed over her brown IYSRAC envelope, and Our Ma handed it over to me to read out, I said, dead casual, 'Just another memo from school, about the rebuilding. Says, we're to remain within our own dwelling places till further notice.'

Lucky that Dee can't read yet. Or she might've spotted the mistake.

'Hm,' said Our Ma. 'Call it an education system when they keep on closing the place down. Now in *my* day—'

'I'm just going for the water, Ma,' I said.

The standpipe on our street was dry as a bone. Not so much as a dribble. At first, I thought some ham-fisted resident had gone and turned it off with one twist too many and jammed it.

'No. I reckon it's been locked,' I told Rah, not that he'd know the difference between jam or lock.

'Big. Mine,' he said.

So we went to try the standpipe in the next street. They mark them with a yellow painted H. That's City Sector One's code for Water, so Our Ma says.

The next standpipe was gushing brilliantly. Rah loved it. After I'd filled the buckets I let him splash about. Be good for his ankle, wash it. Give him a bit of fun too. Poor soul. He doesn't get much.

I was thinking it was time to push off home when a

CHAW Monitor turned up in her neat little car. Rah was squirting water all over the place. I thought she'd call a Warden to stop him. But instead she joined in.

'Splendid fun!' she said with a cheery smile as Rah drenched her uniform.

'Yup,' I said. More fool me for thinking I knew better than Dee what donor-seekers look like. Of course they aren't wicked men with mean evil eyes. They can just as easily look like kindly welfare workers with sky-coloured eyes and soft silky manners.

'Having fun, isn't he?'

'Yes.'

'All right, is he?'

'Yes. He's fine. But I'll make him stop now.' I went to turn the standpipe off.

'Looks like he's got a nasty place on his leg. It needs attention. I'll put a dressing on for him.'

The rag bandage had slipped. The raw wound was showing.

The CHAWM went over to Rah. 'Look, dear. Come with me. I'll see to your leg. Put on one of these.' She held out a wrapped sticking plaster to show him.

Rah grabbed it eagerly.

'No, Rah! Don't,' I said. But he tore off the wrapper and popped it into his mouth before I could stop him. Rah'll eat anything. If she'd offered him a stone, he'd have tried to chew it even if it broke his teeth.

The CHAWM was surprised, but quickly offered him another. He spat the first one out and tried the second.

'Come on, Rah, time to go.' I picked up one of the buckets, tried to put the other one in his hand and make him come with me.

'Rah, we've got to go home now,' I begged. I gave up my attempt to make him carry water. I just pulled him along. Why was he always such a dead-weight?

'Blaaaaaaaaaaaaah!' he growled, baring his teeth. Not

71

the co-operative brother but an angry primate. Of course he didn't want to come with me and carry a heavy bucket when he could be going with the nice smiling lady who was offering him surgical dressings.

I tried to make him. I really did. But he was so much taller than me. I couldn't have picked him up and carried him bodily even if he'd let me.

When I let go of his hand, he stumbled after the CHAWM like a lofty gorilla. When they reached her CareCar, he climbed willingly in. She helped him fasten the security belt.

I remembered what Man had said. Transplantations from living donors are 97.3 per cent more successful than from dead ones.

Rah grinned through the rear window, happy as a pig in plaster.

I didn't bother with the buckets. I raced back to the flat and puffed up the stairs. By the time I got home, another of the CHAWMs had beaten me to it. She was standing right there in our kitchen with her sunbeam smile and her glowing white uniform. She was talking about Netta. She was about to pick her up.

'Cute little dot, isn't she?' she said. 'Netta, that's an unusual name, isn't it? What's the origin?'

'No, Ma!' I said, all out of breath. 'Don't tell her anything.'

'Hello, dear,' said the CHAWM to me. 'We're just doing a routine check on the child's health.'

Netta began jerking excitedly. I know they classified her wrong. She was never an Ultra-Ab. She was sharp as a bean, sharp as six beans. You could tell. That look in her eye. She understood. She'd have learned to communicate one day, if she'd been given the right chance.

The CHAWM said, 'The central HAB decided that this foster child should attend Day Nursery.'

'If it's the inoculations you're worried about, she's all up to date. I had them done proper.'

'We would still like to have her in the special Nursery. We believe that some of her dysfunctions could be cured.'

Thank goodness Ma finally sensed that something was up. She bent down and gathered Netta into her arms. 'No thank you, miss. She don't need no curing. We all think she's perfect the way she is, don't we, poppet?'

Netta tossed her wobbly head and rolled back her eyes. A definite yes. Of course she knew how many beans make five.

'Watch out, Ma!' I said. 'She's trying to get her!'

The CHAWM was trying to grab Netta out of Our Ma's arms. But Ma held on tight. They tussled furiously.

'This way, that a way!' Dee cheered.

There was a Tale-Times tale of two women fighting over a baby. The king said the only fair thing to do was to cut the baby in half. One of the women let go. The king said that proved the child was hers.

Now, it was Our Ma who let go her grip. The CHAWM was off down the stairs like lightning. Netta didn't utter a squeak though her eyes were staring as round as saucers over the CHAWM's shoulder. It was Our Ma who did the screaming, a piteous howl as she stumbled across the kitchen, then staggered to the top of the stairs. I pushed her out of the way and sped down. But by the time I reached the ground floor, the CareCar was already turning the corner at the end of the street, with its siren whining.

I raced back upstairs. 'Ma,' I said. 'I got to tell you. Something else bad.'

When I told her about Rah, she went rabid, screaming and fuming. 'You just let him *go*? How could you do that?' she screamed. 'You go and get him back. Now!

Get both of them. Don't come back till you've found them.'

I went to the Community Social Enquiries Reception in Drury Lane. The CSER are never helpful about anything. This time, they were no different from usual. They didn't understand the urgency.

Before I could even go to the reception desk, I had to produce my ID to prove I was a genuine City Sector One resident. The clerk pointed out that my card needed renewing. He sent me to an office on the first floor. Then I was directed down to the basement. Then back up to the third floor. Five different work stations. Five clerks giving out different information.

Netta Peddle? No record that such a child ever existed. Was she registered?

Netta Peddle? Indeed yes, a report in only half an hour ago from Special Welfare Centre, West Sector Eleven, of a child, gender: F, similar to my description, found wandering the Great West Flyover, crying, hungry, and grossly neglected.

'The victim's been transferred to a place of safety,' said the clerk. 'Till an investigation can begin. What did you say your name was?'

I knew it wasn't her. Netta couldn't possibly wander, only loll.

'Why not pop round in the morning, son? Let's keep our fingers crossed. Something might turn up overnight.'

On the wall behind was a pinboard, thickly covered with photos of young children, some in colour, some in blurry black and white. MISSING! said one of the captions. HAVE YOU SEEN THIS CHILD? said another. LAST SEEN HYDE PARK.

The clerk gave me another form to fill in about Netta. But when I said I wanted to fill in one about Rah being missing too, she lost interest.

'Leaving home, that's the normal thing for a young lad to do. Sounds like your big brother's of an age to know his own mind. Wouldn't be surprised if he isn't having the time of his life some place.'

'But he isn't *normal*. He can't look after himself.' I explained about the microcephaly, his brain the size of a pigeon's egg, him not knowing how many beans make five, and all the rest.

'So your family's been unlawfully sheltering a low-grade Ab?'

'Not unlawfully. Of course not. He's fully registered. He's got a place at the SWU.'

'Then if it's all above board they'll see to it, at his SWU. So don't you worry your little head about it. What you should do is pop along home before curfew.'

We were a desolate trio gathered round the soup-pan that evening. Ma, me, and Dee. We didn't even have any Tale-Times.

'It ain't worth the bother,' Ma said.

Dee said, 'Rah Rah gone away. Fly away home. Come back another day.'

'Shut up,' I said. I mind not saying a proper goodbye to Rah even more than I minded about Mr Winkins. And I don't suppose either of them have really gone to the Place of Peace.

14

Dead End

You can survive without eating for days and days. During the Great Conflagration, people managed for weeks.

But you can't live without water.

Our Ma Peddle was practically off her head now. She didn't want us to leave the flat at all. We kept the door barricaded with all the bunk beds.

When she heard me and Dee shifting them out of the way, she begged me not to go out.

'Ma,' I said sternly. 'We have to fetch water or we'll all die. And dehydration's no way to go.'

But more and more standpipes were being locked shut. We had to go right up as far as Monmouth Place to find one still open. We were hurrying back along Long Acre with our two buckets and some scavvied bread when I spotted a CareCar nuzzling its way through the traffic.

'Listen carefully, Dee,' I said. 'Today, we're going home a different way. So stick close.'

Across the open piazza of Covent Garden was longer. But it's safer. It's where the tourists get taken on some of their guided tours. There's always plenty of people about.

Wrong decision. The piazza was almost deserted. There was a new visitor attraction going on down the Strand. The CareCar was going to spot us easy as pie.

'This way, Dee.' We darted sharp right. I hurried us down Floral Street. There's bollards each end. Vehicles can't follow. That didn't bother our chums the CHAWMs. They got out of the car and sauntered along after us.

'Walk faster, can't you, Dee?' I said.

They walked faster. They were definitely gaining on us. They caught up with us and walked alongside. Dee's short little legs were scurrying left-right, left-right.

'Hi there, my dears.' The voice was light and unthreatening.

Dee turned and smiled uncertainly. She knew her street code.

'Who's in such a big hurry then?' One of them stopped in front of Dee, and held out a gentle hand to her. It was pale, smooth, and hairless. She had her latex gloves on.

'Don't touch her, if you please,' I said.

'Now, then. There's no need for you to get agitated.'

The tone was almost reassuring. But the face was disturbing for she pulled her white gauze mask up over her mouth.

'We're not tagged. You can't touch us. We're not vagrants.'

'It's all right. We know who you are. Just keep calm, dear.' When someone's wearing a mask to prevent the spread of disease, you can't see their lips, but you can still see the shape of the mouth moving. 'You'll only alarm the little girl. *She's* not afraid. Are you, dear?'

Dee turned her slanty piggy eyes from me to the Monitor and back, trying to work out what she was meant to do. Was she protected by her low intellect into not understanding?

'If you come one step nearer to me or my sister,' I said, 'I'll begin shrieking and I'll go on till the only way to stop me is to cut my throat.' What a stupidly brave thing to say. I didn't mean it.

'Listen, sonny Jim, you know this is for the good of everybody. So don't make it more difficult than it need be.'

I saw a lone tourist in brightly patterned shorts and a green sun visor, shuffling slowly along as though he'd lost the rest of his tour group. 'Help us please, sir. We don't want to go with these women.'

I don't reckon he understood a word of it. Or maybe he wasn't used to street children daring to speak to him. He went on past us almost as though we were invisible.

I saw two CSWs down the far end of the street. For the first time ever, I tried to attract their attention.

'Fire! Arson! Fire!'

They were easily within hearing. Why didn't they take any notice? If we were in the slightest bit rowdy on the way home from school they used to be running after us.

The taller Monitor placed her hand on my shoulder with friendly authority. I felt her soft slug fingers.

'You can't,' I squealed. 'My family's opted out.'

'Nobody opts out, pet. Every human who walks on legs has the potential to offer the gift of life to another.'

Rubbery hands were squeezing my shoulder. The other smiling Monitor took hold of my arm, fumbled with the sleeve, pulled it back. Two of them. One of me. Useless. I struggled. I was a little louse with six broken legs wriggling on a comb.

'Take it easy. You'll tire yourself. Just a little shot. A nice sedative. Make you drowsy. We don't want you to hurt yourself.' She took the sterile wrapping off a syringe-pak while the other held me.

Dee stood watching, looking paralysed even without a sedative jab. I was about to be drugged out of existence and she waited patiently with her mouth hanging open. Her brain power was as dim as a one watt lamp-light.

'Run, Dee,' I said. 'Run, run, as fast as you can. Run to catch the pat-a-cake man!'

She tilted her dear round face on one side to see if I really meant she was to go running off on her own, just what I'd been telling her she must never do. I nodded.

A moment's hesitation as she wondered what to do about the bucket, then dropped it, turned, and stumbled off.

I took advantage of the distraction, freed one of my hands and began clawing at their faces. I got her mask off. She wore glossy lipstick, fleshy pink. Her teeth were white and even. I twisted her nose, scratched her cheeks and her ears. Then I dashed after Dee.

Dee hadn't got far. She couldn't run any better than she could speak or do Logarithms. Her upper lip was going blue. Gasping. No way could she move fast enough for us both. When she got breathless, she often threw up. She began to slow down. Now she was retching. The pathetic creature couldn't even walk, let alone run. In deep trouble. Getting us both into deep trouble. Her stupid slowness. What a liability.

The CHAWMs were so cool, even Nurse Scratchy Face.

'No, not me, you fools. *I'm* not a Dysfunc. Take her. She's the dappy mongol.'

'We need the both of you, dear. A little DJLDS child and a size twelve liver. Such an honour to do this for one's community. Your name glorified for ever.'

I pushed Dee towards them. May her name be glorified forever.

She seemed to be rooted to the spot. I had to grab her round her middle and, as though she was the human cannonball and I was the dynamite, I flung her with all my force, right at them.

They're not expecting it. All three fall into a thrashing tangle.

I turn. Heart in mouth, I flee.

15

Fly Pad Feet

I race, terrified as a cat out of a bag. A lynx sprinting over hot coals. No stopping to think. No glancing back. In seconds, I can cover the length of the street. My night-lamp eyes search for the soft crevice in which to hide. The warehouses on either side are blank and solid. No open doorways, no yielding alleyways to melt into. Until, just ahead, I see the dark opening to Lamb's Passage.

Put on speed. Except there's a stitch in my side tightening like a wire noose at every step. To stop the pain, stop pounding over cobblestones. No, don't stop. Keep running or they'll catch up.

Legs move like slow-worms in a dream. Lungs ache with panic. Got to reach the dark passage. Keep going.

You wouldn't try and go down there unless you're a complete brain-dead Ab. Not normally. Narrow, unlit, a covered walkway round the back of The King's Arms Freehouse, well-known loitering place for vagrants, solvent-sniffers, and drinkers without permits. Smells of cow gum, pee, alcohol, mouldy bread.

Just the unsavoury cranny I need.

Check over my shoulder. A second's delay. One of them's picked Dee up, brushed her down. Hand-in-hand, kindly and unhurried, leads her towards the CareCar. The other CHAWM is proceeding casually forward, no undue haste. Everything's done so nicely.

Dart into Lamb's Passage. Only there's another knot of figures at the end, blocking the way out, approaching purposefully. Can't make them out against the light. More CHAWMs? Or are they CSWs?

Don't wait to find out. Half-way up the wall of the

stinky passageway there's a small opening. A privvy air-vent. Scramble up the brickwork. Fear makes me agile so that feet and fingers cling like fly pads. Hurl head-first through the tiny square. Knees graze wooden sill. Flight not slowed. Land heavily, elbow first, on cold, solid, protruding edge. Hear the bone crack like a devilled chicken wing. The landing place quivers with a hollow boom. Open my mouth to yelp but let out nothing except a rush of air.

The thick smell's worse than Ma Peddle's washday. Reckon I've thrown myself into a vagrants' den. But as my eyes grow accustomed to the gloom, I find I'm balancing on a steel beer keg. This is the store-room of a licensed drinking house.

The keg's empty and goes on ringing like a drum. I can't make it stop. I can't stop the ringing in my elbow.

The shed's filled with metal barrels and stacks of empty glass bottles. I begin my descent. But there's the sound of slow shuffling footsteps in the alleyway outside. Like a large silent gang. They stop right outside beneath the air-vent.

I crouch where I am, squeeze my sore elbow so I won't cry, hold my breath till my eyes nearly pop out of their sockets.

Why are they waiting out there? Did they see me slither up the wall? Hear me crash on to the barrels? Are they going to storm the shed?

A clear bright voice begins to recite. 'The King's Arms Freehouse, one of our oldest licensed drinking houses, is now a designated Heritage Centre.'

They call them 'Freehouses'. They aren't really free. We weren't allowed in, only tourists with permits.

'Here, you will have a chance to sample some of the bitters, beers, and ales of a bygone age which the simple people brewed from hedgerow flowers called hops.'

Only a thin wall separates me from a gang of sickly

tourists, so close I can hear every falsehood their tour leader feeds them. The good old days! It's like listening to Ma Peddle.

'Londoners of yore whiled away their evenings in merriment and song and this Sector was renowned for its fine tavern singing. Drinking house choirs specialized in madrigals, ballads, and old London street cries.'

A different voice takes over. His speech pattern's clipped and high, a foreign tongue translating. Then back to voice one.

'Now we enter the quaintly named Snug Bar. The inn-keeper will draw for you, direct from the barrel into pewter tankards, a taste of fermented ale. Note the ancient horse brasses adorning the walls.'

One of the visitors has a coughing fit. Another one's wheezing.

'For those currently on medication or dialysis, Sulla Aquis revitalized mineral water is available, in glass or ampoule.'

Applause as the speech is translated, then murmurs of surprise as the guide explains about pork scratchings.

'Owing to the high salt content, we do not recommend visitors to ingest more than a small taste.'

Food, song, drinking, dancing.

I began again to move down from my perch on the keg. But the movement disturbed a bottle. It slid slowly to the floor and shattered like an explosion.

'Ahahaha!' the guide's voice bellowed. 'Sounds like our evening's merry carousing has already commenced!'

So I stopped where I was till I could hear all the tourists were well inside the Freehouse. I was about to begin climbing down when once more there were voices outside, soft and tender, right under the air-vent. So close I could breathe in their sweet scent.

They'd waited till the tour-group was out of the way

before coming after me. If only the stacked bottles would stay still, not slide out and crash to the ground.

'What've you done with the little girl?' one kind voice asked the other.

'She's in the vehicle. She's fine.'

If Dee was the big prize they wouldn't be needing me.

'I don't know why they bother culling these poor little DJLDSs. Might as well SAD them straight away. They're genetically defective.'

'But useful for research. Gerontology. The ageing process.'

'Where's that other nipper got to? The little beggar. We must've frightened him. We shouldn't rush in so fast.'

'Doesn't matter. We've got his number. Can't do better than that. He's from one of those dreadful Ab Mix families. What a way to live.'

'He can't have got far.'

Both voices went silent. They were listening for me. I went on crouching on top of the keg, like a bird frozen to a branch, legs doubled under me, bruised elbow tight to my side. My heart pounding so loud I could hear it thudding inside my chest like a great engine.

'Roll out the barrel! Let's have a barrel of fun!'

The merriment from the Snug Bar saved me.

I heard the siren wail for curfew time. I listened to a chorus of sickly Pacific Rimmers singing old songs they couldn't understand.

I suddenly remembered Callam. At school last month, we'd had to welcome an important tourist arriving from the other side of the earth. He'd come for a heart-and-lungs replacement. His ancestors were from our Sector. We had to sing to him. The song was about a kookaburra sitting in a tree.

'Now, pupils,' Ms Reed had said. 'We're so honoured that he's chosen our school to visit. So let's see if we can

83

fill our throats with laughter to cheer him on his way. Sing, sing, sing, with all our might to make our guest feel well and bright.'

Callam and I roared the words with gusto. But like these Asians croaking away in the Snug Bar, I hadn't a clue what we were singing about. I hadn't a clue what a kookaburra was.

Callam, who read books, said it was a bird who sang.

I stayed perched on my keg like a silent kookaburra in a tree all night long. From time to time, I wondered about pork scratchings. There are so many things I don't know.

16

On the Run

The siren screamed the end of night curfew. I crept out of my hidey-hole, body cramped, smashed elbow throbbing, zigzagged my way like a house-fly from one doorway to the next, watching my back all the time. I was making my way back to Unapproved Temporary Dwelling Place no. 624/11.

The Highway Hygienists trundled by on their sweeper carts, gobbling up grime, water-sprinklers making pretty rainbows as they laid the dust. Smiling CPE workers were out and about with brushes and mops to polish the statues of our heroes of the Great Conflagration. Nobody took any notice of me.

Look, there's nothing to be afraid of, I told myself. Last night, you just got the jitters. Lily-livered, that's you. Be all right today. 'To be afraid is to be weak.' We'd learned that at school.

Over in Trafalgar Square, the CSH were fixing up coloured banners, flapping pennants, bright bunting. It looked fun.

Olde-Style Medieval Pilgrimage flickered the neon lights, over and over, never tiring of repeating the message. Another new entertainment. Morris Dancers were rehearsing on a wooden platform. Jingling tin bells strapped round their knees. This is my Sector, where I belong. I have nowhere else to be except here.

Don't know what I thought I was up to, wandering round like that, admiring the sights like a visitor. Two giant CSWs appeared, out of nowhere, on the pavement in front of me.

'Freeze, little pal!' one of them ordered. 'On the spot. Exactly where you are.'

I stopped. At least it wasn't a pair of sweet-smiling CHAWMs.

They ambled over, grinning, fingering their holsters. 'And just where d'you think *you're* off to, sonny Jim?'

'To fetch water, sir.' Treat servants of public order with respect.

'Not round here you don't, bimbo boy. Trafalgar Square's off-limits to the likes of you at all times.'

'Can't you see there's a big show coming up? Now hoppit.'

'Yes, sir. I do, sir.' Be polite. Don't seem shifty or they'll take you for a vagrant. 'But you see, sir, the community standpipe's been closed in my quarter. Temporary contamination. The Sector water people are working on it now. Diligently. They said I'd find an open standpipe up this way.'

They must've been coming to the end of their shift. They didn't give me any hassle. Didn't even ask to see my ID, let alone wonder why I had no bucket. A lot of CS wardens are dingbat dim. They're mostly ex-cons or dismissed bodyguards.

'Open standpipe? Top of Northumberland Avenue.'

They dismissed me. I strode purposefully off the way they suggested, then slunk off down Villiers Street as soon as I was out of their sight. Under the arches with the drunks it's shadowy, the cobblestones are greasy. A woman offered me a corner on her mattress and a sip from her plastic bottle. It scorched my throat, then made me brilliant and glowing.

'Cleaning fluid,' she cackled, draining it down to the last drop. Then she began prattling about the good old days, just like Ma Peddle did.

'And we had the Mother Church to take care of us in them days,' she said.

Some of the other drunks joined in with their memories of the good old days.

'Ooh, such singing we had with the Mother Church. All day long! Fair took your breath away with the beauty of it. We will now sing hymn number three hundred and ninety-one, that's what they used to say.'

'And such elegant praying. Let us now pray.'

'And the red wine flowing. The Blood of our Lord.'

'And the Tale-Times! This is the word of God. And what words that God had.'

'And soft white bread baked every day. First the singing. Then the bread. This is the Body of our Lord.'

'And bluebirds in blue skies.'

'Birds? Naw. You're getting the lad muddled. Them was the angels.'

They spoke as though there was a real perfect place that they were going to find their way back to. But even if it was true, none of the drunks were fit to stand, let alone lead the way to their happy-ever-after land.

Their present life-style was the only one that made sense. Drink yourself into oblivion and blow the consequences. Which are inevitable. To be recycled into someone else sitting on a higher branch of the hierarchy tree.

The cleaning-fluid brilliance in my bloodstream didn't last. When I woke, I had a raging thirst, a flashing headache. The drunks had all disappeared. My turn next. Even if the CS Wardens don't get me, the CHAWMs have my number. If I go back to Ma Peddle's, they'll pick me up any time they want. I don't stand a chance.

I nicked some more cleaning fluid off a Highway Hygienist's sweeper cart. For three days I managed to live rough. Or perhaps it was four. Or two. Drinking green slime from drains to slake my thirst. Hiding in skips. I was afraid all the time.

17

Dark Comfort

Dizzy with hunger, drying out with thirst. Cleaning fluid's no good though the hunger you get used to. But you got to have liquid intake. Otherwise the whole system starts to close down. Kidneys, liver, nervous system, circulation, till you can't even stand on your own two legs.

So I'm hauling myself along the ground like a newt. Can't work out where I am. Used to know the sector like the palm of my hand. But now I can't see properly, can't think. Turning into one of those pathetic low-grade Abs. Can't stand creatures like that.

I've reached the bottom of a wide flight of steps. Leads up to a dirty big building. There's a tower pointing to the sky, what the drunks call the Place of Peace Everlasting. 'Course I know it. This is one of the old worship-churches, historic Heritage Centre, number 5. Long ago, citizens, all castes welcome, gathered in them to think about Mother Church. Part of the tourists' trail now. Entrance fee: 100 R. The ancient outside walls are streaked with sky-dirt. Maybe it's sprayed on. Tourists like their history with a touch of grime.

Here's a party of them, waxy-skinned, weary-eyed, with their guide, and servant porters, and medi-nurses, all slung about with oxygen masks, and carri-bags of drugs and IV solutions. Some of them look very sick. Perhaps their received goods haven't been successful. Sloppy surgery. Insufficient tissue-typing.

Tourists carry neat little drink bottles around too, sparkling water, fresh pressed mango juice, golden glucose liquid. Never finish them, just drop them half-sucked on the ground. I'm parched. That's what I'm after.

So I'm crawling up the steps to see what they've left me. Fuzzy eyes, half functioning, spot the nippy CareCar, two CHAWMs in the front, zipping through the swirling traffic on a body-forage. Don't think they've seen me. But any second now.

Blurry vision sees uncollected refuse heaped outside Heritage Centre No. 5. Slither to it. Speedy worm get under that garbage.

So nearly there. Then I'm pounced on from behind. Not squeaky clean CHAWMs but a tall dark figure stinking of rot and yellow dirty flesh. I don't shout. The CHAWMs will hear. He wears a cape, long flapping skirts. He's grabbed me round the middle, flung me over his shoulder. Right by my face is a grizzled chin, foul breath, a mouthful of cracked teeth.

'One more for the pot,' he laughs. 'Even if it's only a tiddler.'

His swivelling eyes log everything. He sees the CareCar slowing down in front of the building. He's leaping up the steps, two at a time, straight in, pushing through the gabbling gawping tourists.

The guard at the entrance desk knows him, waves him in without paying, takes no notice of me slung over his back. I struggle feebly and hammer his shoulder with my fists but it's useless.

We're into the big hall. Tall windows with coloured glass. We're hurrying across, past wooden benches facing to the end like school. There's the table. Dangling from the wall above, an awesome sight. So horrible it frightens some living daylights into me. I struggle and yelp.

The thing is mounted high. There's no avoiding it. A statue. It's no hero cast in metal. An ugly body crudely scratched from wood. Thin, lonely, sad. No clothes, except for the rag round its hips. His arms are outstretched. He thinks he can fly like a bluebird. He's pegged on two pieces of crossed wood. There's a slash in his side, painted shiny red. It looks like it's dripping. He's in bad shape. What's he there for? Symbol or warning?

I know what this place is all about. A theatre of transplantation. It must be. But why is it so dim and dusty? No equipment. No beds. No freezer chests for storage. Not so much as a water tap for a surgeon to rinse his hands. This is where they do illegal trade. Any moment Bedford Peddle 67/9904/BAGF will be no more. I knew all along I was due for SAD. But this isn't how I thought it'd be. I'm lonely and sad like the wooden man on the wall. This place is dirty and undignified.

'Put me down. Leave me!' I whimper.

The trapper grips more tightly with his long crackly fingers.

'Just you be quiet, can't you?' he hisses. 'I'm in charge. So let's have no more of your cheeping.'

'Don't hurt me,' I plead. 'Please.'

'In heaven's name!' He pushes me through a low door, down steep narrow steps, then drags me down a dark passage.

Why doesn't he get on with it? By now I'm jabbering with terror. 'Is this the clinic? Is this where you do it? Where you take them out? How long does it take? Please be quick. Does it hurt? Give me a sedative first. Please don't let it hurt.'

'Don't be such a fool. I don't hurt you any more than I have to. If you stopped struggling I wouldn't hurt at all.'

He thrusts me into a pitch-black space and I hear his running footsteps leaving, then a distant scraping of a lock turning and I know he's left me alone in the dark void. I quiver on the ground and I cry and I cry.

Ever the gutless skunk.

It's a long time before he comes back. By candlelight he washes me. Icy water in a tin basin, not gently but at least it's quick. I'm as thirsty as a guppy on dry land. I drink my bath water.

'All skin and bone, you sad little sparrow. Nothing worth taking out of you except intestinal worms.'

As he dries me with a strip of cloth, he inspects my body all over. What does he want? Who does he think he is? I try to pull away. But he's a whole lot bigger than me. I'm too feeble to resist. Next, he's counting my hurts and marking them in a notebook.

'See, this duckie little book's like my poor old brain,' he says, showing me the page where he's written all about me. 'Holds everything I need to know. Got a memory like a sieve. That's why I write it down. About you, and man's foolishness and God's infinite wisdom. The full works. So what've we got first? Fractured elbow. You'll not be wanting a useless arm for the rest of your life, will you? I'll try and splint that for you, if you'll let me without biting me. Then rickets. Ringworm. Some nasty little jigger bites. Better get rid of them for a start.' He smears something greasy on to the swellings. That's where blow-flies laid eggs under my skin.

'Hold still, can't you? Even little sparrows need a bit of looking after now and then.'

I know he's chiefly checking to find where I'm tagged. 'So no tag then?' he says when he finds I'm not. 'Well, Alleluia and praise to the Lord! That's something to rejoice in. Have to get those out straight away, don't we? Not a nice business. Worse than jiggers. So where've you been hiding out? Down on the riverbank, was it?

Thought you'd be safe in the chasm between the Sectors? That's where most of them are.'

When he's done with his body inspection, fixed my arm, and helped me back into my clothes, he lays both hands on the top of my head and mutters some mumbo-jumbo stuff. I don't understand a word of it. He says he's giving me the blessing of the Lord. At least it doesn't hurt, whatever it is.

Then he offers me a bowl of something grey, cold, and sticky.

'Oatmeal porridge. Eat it if you can, brother. You'll never make it all the way if you're so thin.'

What's it to him if I'm fat or thin, unless he's planning on eating me.

'I'm not your brother, never,' I tell him.

'Are we not all brothers and sisters under the skin?' he says as he takes up his stub of candle and leaves me. In the dark, I wolf down the gluey mixture.

Sensory deprivation is confusing. He's doing it on purpose. I can't tell day from night. Not at first. But I make myself grow used to it. I'm not going to be confused. I won't let him beat me. I discover I'm in a cellar with cold stone walls. One time, I wake from a doze and hear whispering, rustling, and tapping. There must be other captives down here in the dark.

I feel my way along a labyrinth of low passages. The maze is huge, must reach out beneath a dozen or more of the streets of City Sector One. I feel my way, palm by palm, to a larger cellar. A metal grille is set in the roof. It's open to the world above. The soles of people's boots pass overhead.

In the dim bluish light, I make out several small people hunched on the ground. One's rocking himself backwards and forwards. Another's groaning and gnawing his forearm. So this is where the other prisoners are kept.

One speaks to me.

'Welcome,' he whispers, then startled, 'Wow, it's Bedford Peddle!' He stands up and reaches out both arms to hug me. The prisoner knows my name.

'So what if I am?' I pull back.

'Bedford Peddle. Sixty seven stroke ninety-nine zero four stroke BAGF. Unapproved Temporary Dwelling Place, just off Leicester Square.'

He knows my ID too. And my address.

'I *am* glad you're here. I haven't a clue what to do with this lot.' He nods his head at the group of unhappy dwarfs huddled on the ground. 'They're all mute. You've more experience with that sort of thing.'

I recognize his voice even though I can't see his face properly. It seems like light years ago we were sitting next to each other in class.

'Old Callam Six-Toes?'

'That's me.' He giggles. 'Still got the toes. Still breathing, by the skin of my teeth.'

'What in heck are you doing down here?' Even if he'd got the deformed feet, at least he had a real Mum and Dad to watch out for him.

'Same as you.'

'But you can't be! You're HC A-Class. Posh parents. You live in the Residencies.'

'Not any more, brother. They dumped me.'

'The Residency Councillors?'

Worse than that. The people who begot him dumped him.

So Callam told me his tale, quick and quiet, while the other midget prisoners rocked, or slept, or crooned to themselves.

'You remember those brown letters some of us got?'

Of course I did. A girl whose funny little face I didn't want to remember, whose name I didn't ever want to think about, got one. So did a pea-brained youth. And a

93

CP baby. And so would the old woman if she'd not been sightless, and hardly worth the bother of them sending one.

'Mine said I'd got to be tagged. So I'd be available for tissue-matching. They want HIQs. They think it works better.'

I remembered how the old woman argued for the CP's right to live her twisty little life. If she, a false mother, was angry, Callam's parents must have gone ape.

'Sssh. Keep your voice down. You're dead right they were angry. Steaming stonking furious. Dad said why should any Sector get the benefit when he was the one who'd worked his back off rearing me? Mum tried to protect me. She always has. But her obligation's with him, not me. Dad won. So mean he wouldn't sell even a square centimetre of skin till he'd found a bidder for the lot. All at once. Worth more. Greater chance of success. My oesophagus. There's a boy-king in the Andes needs it. 100,000 R.

'When my dad took me swimming in the Residency Club, I thought it was to help my walk. Wrong. Building up my lungs. Better lungs. Bigger price.'

'So he changed his mind?'

'No way. I got away. My sister found out. Got jealous. All the food supplements given to me. She said, Get yourself lost. So I did. Left. Double quick.' He looked down at his boots. 'So that's me. And what about you?'

There's no way I can tell him. My tale is bad, bad, too bad.

I said, 'So they chucked you out? The nipperman got you instead?' Seemed like his luck was a whole heap worse than mine.

18

Blood Money

'He's a whole heap bigger than us. So how do we get ourselves out of here?'

Callam said, 'We don't. You got him wrong. He's taking care of us.'

'But we're prisoners down here.'

'It's a sanctuary. Always has been. For years, even before all the Conflagrations. When people were in trouble, they hid under worship centres. Don't you see? He's going to save us. Reckons he can get a whole group away. So far, there's me, and the five he rescued from the Personnel Transporter. Now you. That's seven. He'll find another three or four and we'll be off. He's got it worked out.'

'And what's in it for him?'

'Nothing. Why should there be?'

'Nobody does anything for nothing.'

'Father Gregory's our brother. He's not alone. There's people all over the sectors doing this kind of thing.'

'What for?' Collecting misfits doesn't make sense.

'For love, brother.'

So Callam's swallowed all that brother-love make-believe. He wants to call me brother too.

'I'm not anybody's brother,' I tell him. 'Belong to myself. Full stop.'

The other five are all DJLDS boys. They're chunky, with short limbs and no necks. In the dim light, I see the slanting eyes beneath epicanthal folds, the snubby noses, round moonbeam faces, the splayed spatulate fingers.

For all his brother-love beliefs, Callam's wary of

them. Not quite afraid, but he keeps his distance. He doesn't like them touching him, specially the shambling bearlike one who keeps reaching up and trying to put his arms round him.

Callam's been cooped up with them for over two weeks but he still can't tell them apart. He thinks they're test-tube products.

'They've been cultivated for their parts,' he says. 'They're identical. They've all got the same squinty eyes. Like peas from the pod.'

''Course they're not! They may be DJLDSs, but they're not all the same. They're completely different. They're not even brothers.' Even in the half-dark you can tell. 'They're Down's people. You just think they're the same because you're not looking at them properly. It's a myth that all Trisomy 21s look the same.'

'Trisomy? You mean like your little sister?'

'I haven't got a sister. They're like themselves.'

4590BN7888MNS349/B was never like these boys. She was High Grade. She could speak, follow instructions, sing, dress herself, tell shaggy dog stories. These poor little fellows are so Low Grade they're almost sub-human. Perhaps they could've made it up to Middle Grade if anybody had bothered to help them to help themselves.

One of them, perhaps the eldest, he looks about fourteen, continually rocks himself backwards and forwards. He stops only to growl or grunt or to reach out and try to hug Callam. Another examines shreds of wool he's pulled from his blanket. Then he eats them.

He reminds me of the beanpole. Thinking of Rah makes me start to choke. Nobody's going to see me cry.

I stare at the wool-gatherer who stares at his hands, then laughs. He's found his own hands and recognized them!

'Look, Callam,' I can't help saying. 'That one knows

96

he's got hands. He's playing with them. And his fingers. It's a very good sign.'

The third boy is using his hands to try to communicate with Callam. There's a gleam of brightness in his tiny eyes. He's using some kind of sign language. But I don't know it, so I can only smile and nod.

The fourth sits hunched in a vacant stupor, dribbling, tongue lolling out, facing the damp wall without seeing it, responding to nothing. Old Peddle didn't like it when 4590BN7888MNS349/B hung out her tongue. She said it made her look like a cretin. 'Put away your tongue, Devon,' she used to say. 'Or I'll think you're asking for it to be chopped off with the knife.'

The youngest boy's body is so floppy you have to lean him against the wall for him to sit. It's tricky to guess his age. DJLDSs develop slowly. Perhaps he's four. Or six. Or somewhere in between. Without thinking, I start to stroke his cheek like I used to stroke Netta's. But he doesn't notice. I can hear, inside my head, Old Peddle's angry voice. For crying out loud, she's saying. What a disgrace! Neglecting them like this! And she'd smother them in whiskery kisses.

'I'm sorry, brother, if I upset you,' says Callam uncertainly. 'Expecting you to do what I can't. I thought that with your, you know, your experience, you'd know what to do about them.'

'Then you thought wrong,' I tell him. I don't want to get involved. I just want to get away.

The priest returns. He pats us on our heads.

'So my little sparrows have found one another?' he says. 'God bless.'

He's brought food. He doesn't stay long. He's off again without stopping to eat.

The two youngest prisoners can't even feed themselves. They're too dim. Or too distressed. Or nobody's bothered to teach them yet. Callam's been putting food in front of them, and wondering why they don't take it.

'You're a dysfunctional fool,' I tell him. Reluctantly, I put a spoon into each flabby hand. Then I must lift the hands towards the droopy mouths. It takes a long time. But eventually, they'll learn to shovel up their own gruel.

'Dysfuncs don't learn fast. And they don't learn by themselves. But they learn most things in the end, if you give them time.'

'Thanks, brother.'

'I told you. I'm not your brother.'

Each time the priest returns, he brings a pocketful of scavvied food. Mouldy oatmeal one day, soft rotting potatoes the next. Each time we see him, his breath smells worse, his face is paler, his big protruding eyes more yellow. He walks unsteadily on his big flat feet. Yet even when he's so breathless that he's scarcely able to speak, he places his hands on the top of each of our heads and mutters his mumbo-jumbo words.

'It's a blessing,' Callam tells me.

There must be something in it because the DJLDSs seem to respond to his touch. Even the big lad who spends all his waking hours rocking and chewing at his own flesh stops and looks up when it's his turn for the mumbo-jumbo.

'That's no ordinary Ab-Dab,' I say. 'That's a mighty unhappy kid.'

The priest raises his hands over my head. It's my turn for the bla-bla-bla. I put up with it for the sake of the others. The sleeves of the priest's black cassock fall back. I catch a glimpse of blue bruise puncture marks the length of his arm.

This man is a serious abuser! He has been storing us muttonheads here to fatten us, to sell us to buy his gear.

I'm so angry. Not with him. But with myself. Why didn't I crack it sooner?

'He's going to use us all,' I yell into the dark passage as the priest sweeps away on his evening scavvy.

Callam calms me. 'No, brother, it's the other way.'

'Don't you brother me!' I scrape his hand off my shoulder.

'Then keep your voice down or you'll give us all away. Father Gregory's selling himself for our sake.'

How can I believe what Callam tells me? It's a make-believe. The priest goes out to sell plasma in the night-market to buy food.

'It isn't true, Callam.' He could donate once a month if he was a fit man. The body renews itself. But he's just a bag of bones. 'Nobody in their right mind would risk their life like that day after day.'

'Unless he loves his fellow man more than himself,' says Callam.

'Huh. You wouldn't catch any sane person doing anything as stupid as that. He's either mad or an idiot.'

When Callam Six-Toes tells me that the final refuge the priest is sending us to is the real Mother Church, I can't believe this either.

'It's not even a place. Just an idea in gullible people's minds.'

'But it's both!' says Callam. 'A living idea *and* a living place. Mother Church is home on earth and a sanctuary beyond the Great Divide. And Father Gregory's brothers there welcome all poor and dispossessed people. For that is their way. Love is the fulfilling of the law.'

When our priest returns with the handful of weevilled rice bought with his life-blood, lies down to rest, and dies in his sleep, I know he's been a fool. And so have I for not getting out of here sooner.

19

Reverend Father Rests in Peace

Callam wasted precious body fluid. He wept wet tears.

Not me. I've seen stiffs before, plenty of times. Vagrants, drunks, druggies, rolled on their backs in the gutter, terror chalked on their faces.

The pale priest's expression was calm.

I said, 'So he can't have been scared. Perhaps he didn't know he was on the way out.'

Callam snuffled. 'There wasn't anything for him to be scared of. He knew where he was going.'

Callam's weird. First he cries over the corpse, then wants to do some of the mumbo-jumbo praying stuff.

I shrugged. 'Please yourself. If it makes you feel better.'

He moaned strange words to a mournful tune. Soon after, he was scavenging the pockets of the corpse's cassock to find the notebook. He slipped it inside his shirt, right next to his body. For a boy who grew up in the soft security of the HCs, he was doing well at self-preservation.

People were beginning to know we were there. We heard tapping on the other side of the door. We crept along the dark passage and peeked through a knot-hole in the wood.

It was a young woman.

'Dear reverend Father,' we heard her plead. 'Please, for the mercy of God open the door to me.'

I recognized her. She was Lucy, the go-go dancer from Glamour Nites Fun Club. When I used to go out on a scavvy after school, I'd see her lounging in the club entrance beckoning to the tourists. She didn't look glamorous now. She wore the same kind of greasy padded jacket we all had. She looked wretched.

She was holding something. It looked like another jacket, rolled up. Callam whispered, 'Perhaps it's food. For when we shout to the Lord for help, help cometh only from the Lord.'

But it was a baby bundled up. The woman sensed someone was on the other side of the door. She didn't know it wasn't the priest.

'Take him, Father. I beg you. I want nothing for myself. Just save my son. He's blind and deaf with the rubella. They'll use him if they find him. At least he stands a chance with you.'

Callam's hand was already hesitating on the latch. If I hadn't grabbed hold of it with my good arm and bent it back, he'd have opened up and let the woman in.

'You muttonhead,' I whispered. 'This isn't a care centre. It'd be suicide to take in a dysfunctional. Even if it isn't tagged, it'd give us away the minute it started crying.'

The dancer didn't give up. 'Reverend Father, have mercy.'

I put my mouth to the hole in the door. 'The priest is dead!' I hissed. 'Now go away. Get lost.'

But she stayed there pleading and cursing for hours. Luckily, by morning she and the baby were gone.

We had no food. The corpse was beginning to stink. We dragged it as far from the sleeping chamber as we could.

'So it's up to us,' I said. 'To get away as soon as we can.'

Callam showed me the plan. It was complicated. The priest had worked it all out, the disguises we were to wear, the route for smuggling us out of the worship centre and hiding us in the Sector's medieval pilgrim show, the horses from the knacker's yard which would carry us into the eastern sectors. It would be three night's travelling. Every last detail was set down, even the hymns to be sung on the way, and the words of thanksgiving to be recited on our arrival when the bishops welcomed us into the safety of the Mother Church.

Perhaps the priest had been sound after all. 'It's really excellent,' I said.

Callam said, 'Yes, but it won't work. Not without transport, it's too far.'

'We don't need the horses. We've got legs. We follow the map on foot.'

'That's all very well for us two. But what about them?' He meant the five on the floor. 'They'd never manage that long way. The small one can hardly even walk properly.'

'Them?' I said, shocked. I hadn't realized he was daft enough to consider dragging the DJLDSs along too. We hadn't a hope in hell of getting away if he did.

'Brother, they need us.'

'And we don't need them. They're non-productive joeys, Callam. They'll never be able to do anything.'

'They deserve a chance. We are not worthy to live if we don't help them. That's what Mother Church life is all about. Love. And love has no limits.'

He was only saying stuff he'd read up in the notebook. He can't have really believed it.

'Listen, Callam. I *know* about people like these. I've *lived* with them. Their only function is to drag you down. You have to do *everything* for them. I'm telling you, if I get out of here alive, I don't ever intend to live in a collective group with that type again. When I was at the old Peddle woman's squat, who was it always having to do the work for the rest of them? Who

102

was it fetched their water every day? Cleaned the vermin off their heads? Escorted them along the streets? Yours truly.'

'I always admired you for that.'

'It wasn't worth your energy. As for this bunch, they're going to be taking their last gasp soon enough anyway. See this one here?' I pointed to the clumsy bear who rocked himself backwards and forwards. 'See the colour of his lips? Blue. And his skin? All mottled. Don't you understand, Callam? It means he's already sick. Any stress, and it's curtains. Why risk your own skin for someone so weak he's going to die anyway?'

But Callam had the priest's notebook. I could have fought him for it, but with one arm splinted, I'd never have won.

'OK,' I said sulkily. 'So you're the boss. We do it your way.'

'No, Bedford. I can't be the boss and I can't do it alone. We have to be a team. You understand their needs better than I ever will. That's why we have to stick together.'

'Very well,' I said. 'In that case, we go by river.'

Callam's eyes nearly popped out of his head. 'Down the river! We can't. Too dangerous. It's poisoned. There's cholera and rats' piss disease and chemicals and all sorts in that water. What if one of them falls in?'

'You got a better idea then?'

Of course he hadn't. All brotherly love and no realism.

Weird or what? I vowed never again to live in collectivity. Yet already I'm lumbered with this lot, one with six toes to a foot and a domineering nature, another five so dappy they didn't even know their own names.

Old Peddle used to say that even the lowest grade of Multi-Dysfunctional deserved a pre-name of their own.

I said, 'I won't be taking any no-names on my boat. If they're coming too, they got to get names.'

'How?'

'We'll call them Tom, Dick, Harry, John, and Joe. OK?'

20

Foul Water Runs Deep

Callam found the woollen cloaks hidden for us in a niche. He said they would make us look like pilgrims. We pulled the hoods well down over the boys' faces so the special features of their faces would not show. Callam tried to make them keep their heads bent forward and to hold their hands with the palms pressed together.

But hand-speak Harry kept throwing back his head and laughing. He knew this was a game of disguise and make-believe so he was enjoying it.

Callam said, 'I thought you said they could be taught to do things?'

'They can. But slowly.'

'As for you, you've got to be more prayerful. Keep your eyes down, like you're thinking humble thoughts. Don't look so shifty.'

It wasn't shifty I felt. It was scared.

When we heard the crowds gathering in the street above we knew it was time to go up.

Callam muttered some words under his breath, more praying, then turned the creaky lock in the door. My heart was pounding. I took a deep breath. Seven brown dwarfs filed up the steps, shuffled across the worship centre, and out into the shocking whiteness of daylight. We had to stop and blink.

Below us, the square was swarming with entertainers, musicians, jousting horses, sideshows, booths, clog-dancers. John was terrified. If I hadn't kept tight hold of him, he'd have scuttled right back into the dark. The noise of tabors, tambourines, and trumpets was loud and confusing. The tannoys were urging the people to stand back to let the procession through. Some stupid tourists at the back of the crowd thought that meant us. One of them took a photo. Others turned to stare. They all began to stand aside to let us pass down the steps. It was like a path opening. We were urged forward. This wasn't part of the priest's intentions.

Down in the square it was even more dense. You could hardly move for people. There were enough tourists to fill a thousand clinics.

There was no time for eyes down and looking prayerful. We had to keep our eyes skinned or we'd get separated. I lost Harry. The idiot slipped through the crowd to get nearer the fire-jugglers. I grabbed hold of his cowl and hauled him back. Two mongols on my good arm, one on the other. They should be kept on leashes like hounds. Callam had big Tom and dopey Dick. What next?

A tourist right near us was taken with a seizure. He fell to the ground, writhing. Rah used to do it. But you don't often see it in public. The nearby spectators mistook it for a jester's acrobatics and jostled nearer to get a better look. Then the man stopped moving and lay still. A woman saw that the man at her feet had just had a Premature Demise Experience. She became hysterical. Her panic spread.

Paramedics struggled through. A tourist taking a PDE wasn't meant to happen in a public place.

This commotion is just what we need. We get out quick, dragging our dependents between the legs of the crowds.

'Make for the river,' I called and we all ran.

Big Tom's breathless and blue. Dick's jabbering. I grab an abandoned shopper trolley and heave them both into it. I lift up baby Joe and carry him piggyback. Callam must cope with the other two.

We reached Embankment. I scrambled first up the

wall, jumped down the other side on to the slush. Then Callam got up and hauled the others to perch beside him.

'Big drop,' I warned him. 'And slippery.'

He handed them down to me, boy by boy.

Considering none of them knew what the heck was happening, they were co-operative. For once, their docile passivity was a help. Not all DJLDSs are like this. Sometimes they ask bright question, sing songs, tell you their way of doing things, and smile at you with a precious grin that wraps from ear to ear.

No. Don't think about her when it hurts so much. Just concentrate on the ones you've got right here.

Foamy brown wavelets slapped the shore. Across the soup, South Sector Three's lights twinkled in the dusk. Upstream, the west glowed with a fiery sunset and downstream was already being gobbled up by the dark. But somewhere, way down in the blackness, more than twenty sectors distant, lay a tiny chance for us. I felt a lurch of hope. Could we really find Callam's Mother Church and be safe?

Our five dependents began slithering across the refuse. Why are Dysfuncs so drawn to water? The pea-brain beanpole who was never my brother had made right for it too, just as Tom, Dick, Harry, John, and baby Joe were doing. Their robes dragged round under their feet. Any moment, one of them was going to slip over, probably dopey Dick. Sharp-edged rubbish poked through the softer stuff and the place was teeming with rats.

Callam said, 'Can't you keep them still? Tie them down or something?'

'Like animals, you mean?' I said sarcastically. 'Tether them?'

'They're wandering. They'll draw attention to us.' Callam was jumpy as a frog. 'Just do something.'

'Why me? It's *your* fault they're here.'

'They understand you.'

'They'd understand you if you tried a bit harder.'

Callam talks of brotherly love but he still hates having to touch them. But he's right. For their own safety, they must be controlled.

So my first scavvy of the evening was a diesel storage tank lying on its side against the embankment wall. From above, you'd hardly know it was there. The second scavvy was a blue mattress, only a bit stained.

'Lend a hand, Callam, can't you?' I shouted at him. Now I'm getting jumpy.

We dragged the mattress over to the rusty tank and laid it inside. I led our five boys in, made them sit, then blocked the open side with a packing case. They could see out, if they could be bothered, but not get out. They bleated a bit. Then Dick started an in-depth finger inspection, and Tom began to rock himself into a crooning trance. The two younger ones fell asleep. Only Harry folded his short arms across his chest and stared balefully out at me with disapproval.

'OK, so I'm treating you like penned animals,' I said to him, as though he could understand speech. 'But you've got to be safe so we can get on with the craft.'

I scavvied a bit of rotten bread and broke it into five pieces for them.

I'd imagined we'd build a sturdy little boat out of wood, like the Tale-Times ark. I'd told Callam that's what we'd do. But I'd misremembered riverbank pickings as being richer and more varied. There was practically nothing useful left.

I said, 'A raft'd be just as good.'

It was not even a raft, just a piece of white packing material bobbing on the water. I pulled it ashore.

'Doesn't look big enough to take seven,' said Callam. 'It'll have to.'

We set to work reinforcing it with bits of driftwood. We made it more buoyant with extra layers of polystyrene lashed on.

Out of nowhere, a thin voice piped up, 'They're not very well hidden, those joeys of yours, are they? You won't keep them long if you don't cover them properly.' I looked up and for a stupid magic moment, I thought it was Harry speaking. Of course it wasn't. It was a younger boy, barefoot, naked except for a blanket. He'd been poking around the oil tank. He was armed with a stout stick with a nail through the top.

'Leave them alone!' I shouted.

He had a long scar in his side, stretching right round to his back. It hadn't healed tidily.

He saw me stare. 'Yep,' he said. 'They got me. They get you ever?'

I said, 'You leave our friends alone! They're not doing any harm!'

'Never said they were. But anybody could find them if they tried. You should rough up the camouflage. Cover them in weeds or mud. That's if you don't want someone to swipe them.'

Who did this small boy think he was to give me advice?

'Push off,' I said, wishing I had a weapon. He moved off, keeping close to the shadow of Embankment wall, poking at the ground, stopping and crouching to scavvy with the spiked end of his stick.

A SASPK would suit me primo. Twenty blades for cutting, slicing, skinning, protecting the weak. Some hope of finding one. The riverside's been scavvied too often. Instead, I found an umbrella frame, wiry like a burned-out ribcage. I'll sharpen the tip with a stone.

When Callam saw it, he wasn't impressed. 'Blessed be the peace-makers,' he said. He's getting more cryptic.

The raft was as ready as we were going to get it. We loaded our watercan, our small bag of vegetable roots, then the five boys. As each one was settled in his place, our raft sank lower. More water slopped on board.

Then, suddenly, out of the darkness came a surge of tiny children, screaming and waving their arms, and scattering the rats. We were being stormed by a straggle of waifs, small ones carrying even smaller ones on their backs. They swarmed round us, scrabbling to get on to the raft, to pull the five boys off. Their faces were scabby and their bodies covered with yellow scar tissue. Already our craft was overladen. One more and we'd all sink.

'Buzz off. Go away!'

But they're stubborn. They won't back off. I push off with the umbrella and Callam paddles frantically. The grubby urchins are following us into the water. Don't they know about cholera?

I grabbed the umbrella like a spear and made stabbing movements at one of them who was trying to push John into the water. She toppled backwards and disappeared under the surface. She came up spluttering and made for the shore. John was whimpering with terror.

We managed to push away from the putrid shore. The Electric Night-Light Show was starting. You could hear the distant music. And then watch the pin-prick fantasy lights spangling like stars, and the eerie arc-beams cut through the black like knives. Then the searing phosphorous white illuminates all the Sector buildings, before the full spectacle of the aurora borealis shimmers in coloured curtains of light across the open sky.

The DJLDSs stared up, transfixed. Five mouths gaping like little fishes. Five pairs of eyes staring like bluebottles. The night show is so beautiful. The place we were leaving behind is so vile.

I could hear a little girl's voice chanting inside my head.

That a bad bad place. Go away. Get away.

21

Downstream

But we weren't moving forwards. The river was choked solid. We were jammed on all sides by rubbish.

'Thought you said you knew about rivers,' Callam said angrily. 'You should've thought to make us a sail.'

Typical HC. Full of good ideas too late.

'So should you,' I snapped.

A CPE night patrol launch passed quite near. But we're so low in the water, it didn't even notice us there. We're just another blob of flotsam. Next, it's a chopper circling lazily overhead. Searchbeams roving like a white sword. Stupid John came out of his vacant stupor and waved merrily upwards. Callam got jumpy again.

'It's no good,' he said. 'They've seen us. I *knew* this plan was useless.'

'I didn't notice you come up with a better one. Anyway, they're not interested in us. I told you before. They're after bigger fish. Now stop worrying and start rowing.'

The chopper did us good. The whirlwinding blades dispersed some of the rubbish. We paddled hard. We got to a clearer part of the river where the water was flowing sluggishly. Then, without warning, we were seized by a strong current. We were hurtling forwards as though we had an outboard motor. Past warehouses, docks, cranes, the empty barracks, the half-submerged hulk of a submarine. We weren't really going any faster than a pedicab. But being so close to the surface it seemed like it was full steam ahead.

Polystyrene's flimsy stuff, too frail for a raft. All the time we were skimming through the water, crumbs kept breaking off and fluttering away like snowflakes in the night.

'Watch it!' I yelled at Callam. Too late. We thumped into something solid. It was an unlighted buoy. Bits of our raft at the side tore away, making it a square metre smaller, and riding lower. I was worried. If any more chunks broke away, there wouldn't be enough buoyancy to keep all of us afloat. But then, Harry fell asleep, slumped sideways, and before we could grab him, slipped off the raft. Slowly, he went down in the rubbishy water with his eyes wide open. He didn't shout or cry. It was as though he understood exactly what was happening to him.

For a moment I thought baby Joe must have understood too. 'Bye bye bye bye,' he babbled. I didn't even know he could speak. But perhaps his bye-byes didn't really mean anything.

It was the most stupid accident. And why did it have to be Harry? The strongest and brightest of the five who might have had a chance to make something of freedom when he got it? Why not big Tom with the ropy heart who wasn't likely to survive the journey anyway? Or dopey Dick who did nothing except stare at the stubby fingers on his squat hands?

'I told you we should've *tied* them,' Callam wailed.

'We shouldn't even have brought them at all.'

They should've had a quick SAD, been put out of their sufferings. We're all going to drown anyway. Callam's the only one who can swim.

Callam did some of his mumbo-jumbo praying in the direction that Harry disappeared. Then, moving gingerly, we shoved the remaining four to a slightly safer position in the centre of the raft. They clung to one another. Had they, despite their pigeon-brains, understood something of our grim situation? Callam and I re-positioned ourselves facing inwards so we could keep an eye on them all the time. One fewer passenger, and we're riding a little higher.

113

So we're still bobbing downstream. All through the night. Fast for a while, then slow. Now lurching and spinning, whirling on an eddy till we feel sick. It's like we're sucked down a nightmare tunnel, not knowing what's in the dark on either side.

We see an orange glow of faraway fire on the land. Callam says it's one of the New Age settlements in the outer sectors. He might be right. We're clinging to our flimsy raft like flies on a broken egg shell. My head nods down to my chest. Glory be. I'm dozing off. The relief of sleep.

But then I dream. I'm with a sweet girl. I'm handing her to the woman in white. Then the dream re-starts. Now we're playing on the street, the girl and I. I'm telling her Tale-Times. I'm making her finish her cabbage soup. I'm tying red ribbons in her hair. I can't get her out of my head.

'Bedford!'

She's calling me. Help me.

'Bedford!'

And I'm flinging her like a stuffed dummy to the smiling monitors.

'Brother Bedford! Wake up! You can't sleep now!'

Have to keep awake. Make sure no one else slips overboard.

Callam tells stories, one after another. Anything to keep us holding on. There's angels, and kings, camels, long journeys by land and sea. Floods, beggars, babies slaughtered and babies born to be God. He's not making them up out of his head. Everybody knows them. They're Mother Church Tale-Times.

At last, blackness softens to grey. The beginning of dawn. We can make out the pale glow of one another's hands and faces. We can see the dark stripe of land. And we can see there's only five of us. Another of the boys has slipped off and we didn't even notice. It was little Joe. Bye bye baby.

Now it's my turn to waste precious body fluid on tears.

I wail and sob and swear. 'It's all pointless. I can't go on with this.'

'You can! Look, we're nearly there!' says Callam. 'Please, we've got this far. Don't let go now.'

There's a bit of sandy beach in sight, with tussocky dry hills above it.

Callam says, 'You've done brilliant, to get us this far. If you sit tight, the tide'll pull us in.'

The nearer we get to that barren burned-out land, the more excited he becomes. The sun comes up red.

'Yeah, I have seen a great light!' Callam calls.

I can see blackened tree stumps and he's praising God for them too. He's shouting Alleluias into the sky and he turns to grin at me and sees the great container ship, stacked high with crates, as tall as a ten-storey building, as long as a city block, bearing down on us. We wave. We scream. We shout. Nobody on board up there can possibly see us in time.

As we capsize, Callam yells instructions. 'Hang on to Tom! I'll take the other two!' Callam's HC. Of course he knows how to swim. But I don't.

'Lie on your back!' he shouts. The raft is breaking up in the water all round. 'Don't panic! Relax like you're in the bath!'

Who does he think I am? I've never seen a real bath.

'Kick! Kick hard. That's all there is to it.' He makes it seem easy.

But we're overboard. In the water. Under the water and struggling to breathe and drowning and I can't hear what he's saying any more. Green bubbles before my eyes. Bubbles inside my ears. And I know the one thing I must do is cling tight to Tom as he drags me down deeper. Or do I drag him? Who is clinging to who? One Dysfunctional drowning another.

Drowning is too hard to do. The man we scavvied dead from the riverbank so long ago, he didn't drown either.

The old woman once said, 'An eggcupful of water'll drown you if you want it to. Or you can survive the oceans of the world. It's up to you, Bedford.'

And the next moment, Tom and I, still clinging to one another, are plucked out of the sea by a long hooked pole. We're swinging through the air like flying fish. I see the little rowboats winched down from the big ship and one of them veers off course to reach us. We're landed in the bows, gasping and retching. Tom's sprawled on his back beside me, not moving.

I've failed. I'm alive. He's dead. Then he opens his piggy eyes, pulls himself upright till he's half sitting, leans forward, puts his short little arms round my neck and squeezes so hard it hurts.

'Bath.' He gives a watery chuckle in my ear. 'Bath. Bath!' His first word. His first joke.

I feel a tightening in my chest so that I want to hug him back. But I mustn't let myself feel anything for anyone again. I unfasten his arms and push him away.

The sailors save Callam, Dick, and John too, then get on unloading the big ship into the rowboats. Then ferrying cargo to shore.

'Mind your backs. Bishops' provisions,' a sailor tells us and another crate is lowered on board.

Pineapples Sierra Leone is stamped on the side. I read all the labels. Mussels from New Zealand, lobsters from the New World, strawberries from Spain. Fermented juices from Burgundy. Ortolans and Chinese lotus flowers in ginger syrup. Widgeon wings in calvados. We are going to a world of plenty.

'Pilgrims?' asks the sailor. 'Must be your lucky day. I'll put in a word for you with the foreman.'

We reach land. There's a line of trucks waiting. Our sailor goes to the head of the convoy, speaks to the driver, gives him something from his breeches pocket. The driver nods. He's accepting it. And so we find ourselves quickly transferred into the back of the truck, balancing on the crates.

It's a bumpy ride along the New Pilgrims' Way as it winds across burned-out heathland. Tom's forgotten he spoke one word and made a joke. He's back to his pointless rocking. Dick's whimpering. John's gnawing his fists. We're all hungry and we're all drying up with thirst. I catch the fragrant honey scent of pineapples packed inside the crates on which we perch. See, smell, sit on but do not taste.

Callam stands up and peers ahead. He begins to shout. 'I can see it! It's really there!'

On the faraway horizon, shimmering in the haze, rising up through it, is a white ancient city.

Callam begins to sing and tears pour down his cheeks. 'O shout to the Lord in triumph! Serve the Lord with gladness! Come before his face with songs of joy!' He wants me to join in.

Dick begins to howl. Can he know better than Callam what's waiting for us, that there'll be no open arms to welcome us into paradise?

22

The Place of Milk and Honey

The lead truck swerved abruptly into the bank, avoiding an obstacle in the way. We practically slid off the back. It was a group of children pushing a handcart, straggling along in the middle of the track.

The whole convoy shuddered to a halt. The children scattered to one side. Callam called down a greeting. They were refugees from another of the city sectors, a scruffy bunch, but with such bright hope in their faces. Two stringy young boys were loping along on either side of a sightless youth. I saw the red tag-scar on his ankle. Quite recent. Not healing properly. There was a pair of twins too, conjoined at the hip, and a young mother with a tiny baby tied in a shawl on her back. Six in all, or seven if you counted the twins separately, though there's only one pair of legs between them.

The trucks started up again. We thundered past the walkers in swirls of dust. The girl-mother glanced up, irritated, scowling, pulling her scarf over her mouth. I knew the criss-cross lines of her frown. I recognized that angry toss of her head. My heart stopped moving. It was her. My own family.

I scrambled over the crates to the rear of the truck. I would've jumped down, except that Callam held on to me too tightly. 'Watch the wheels, Bedford! You'll be scrunched into slurp!' The next truck was close behind.

'Pica, Pica!' I screamed and the girl glanced up. So I knew it wasn't her. Pica wouldn't have heard. The girl half-raised one hand in a wave and her eyes above the scarf smiled. Of course it wasn't Pica. It was just a trick of the light shining through the dust.

The Mother Church is protected within the double-walled city. You come first to the outer perimeter. This is a tall fence of steel, hooped along the top with razor-wire. This is where the convoys have to stop and trucks are unloaded. Everybody has to walk the rest of the way, unless they're the bishops.

It wasn't far, just across the gravel to the inner wall. This is built like a castle, from massive blocks of stone, with look-out turrets all round. There are sturdy wooden gates carved with winged figures. Here, visitors quietly queued for admittance.

So we joined the end of their line. Callam gazed with awe at the gold-tipped spires of the sacred centre on the other side of the walls. You could see green fluffy tree-tops waving in the wind. There was the mysterious tolling of bells and the sound of strange singing. I didn't see angels or bluebirds but all the tourists who emerged, clutching their bright tinsel relics and pretty paper souvenirs, were smiling.

At last, we reached the head of the queue. But the gatekeeper wouldn't let us through.

'This isn't a public park for riff-raff, you know,' he growled.

'But we're pilgrims,' said Callam.

'So where's your pilgrim passes?'

Every other visitor had a day ticket ready to show.

Callam said, 'All right, so we're not real pilgrims. We're the poor and dispossessed who, so it is written, shall inherit the earth.'

The gatekeeper scowled. 'You mean you got worker permits?'

Of course we hadn't.

'Guest workers, pilgrims, acolytes, servants, whatever it is you are, then you got to have your permits,' said the gatekeeper wearily.

We weren't any of those.

The gatekeeper scratched his beard. 'So what are you then? Because the Dean and Chapter don't care for any admittance irregularities.'

John, bored and frustrated with chewing his arm, began to bang his head rhythmically against the wooden gates, then laughed at the sound it made.

The gatekeeper said, 'Had a son like that myself. Long time ago. Look, I'll consult the book. They may let you become Friends.' He retreated into his keeper's lodge for a moment.

'That's it. Official Friendship of the Mother Church entitles you to make financial donation towards upkeep of external fabric. Plus free admittance to special Feast Day celebrations.'

I said, 'We can't make donations. We don't have money. We don't even have food.'

The gatekeeper sighed. 'Not up to me, is it? I'm only a common mortal doing my job. Though if you want my advice, you'll leg it, back to wherever you come from. You won't find there's room for you here. And you're not the first to try it on either.'

Callam tugged me away. 'He doesn't know anything, Bedford. Come on. Let's wait till we can talk to one of the priests. Let the children come to me, that's one of their mottoes. I know it's going to be all right. Maybe they'll send the Archbishop out to bless us.'

The gatekeeper overheard. 'His holiness? Out here?' he laughed. 'You must be joking. He's the real big cheese. You won't catch *him* out here.'

Callam said we'd wait anyway.

The warm morning wore on. The gatekeeper grew grumpier. So many foreign visitors arrived. All to have their passes checked. The sky overhead buzzed with air-cabs, arriving and departing. Sometimes they were stacking five and six high, waiting for their turn to land.

But still we weren't admitted, nor did anyone from the Mother Church come out, though from time to time one of the foreigners threw some coins, or raised a camera. Callam kept reassuring me that he knew in his bones it was going to be all right because he'd been praying hard.

About midday, the six refugees (or seven depending on how you counted the conjoined twins) we'd passed earlier turned up. There was no welcome for them either. We let them share the triangle of shade we'd found beside the buttresses of the city walls. They still had some provisions left. They shared them generously. It was flakes of dried saltfish.

The younger ones slept. We waited. At dusk, the gates were pulled shut and secured with iron bars. I'd expected nothing. It was no surprise to find nothing. But Callam was slain.

Some of the others, the two loping CPs, the curious twins, the girl-mother, began softly to clap their hands. 'Hosanna, Hosanna!' they sang. It was a beautiful sound they made. But I didn't believe that merely saying the right word could make things better. Callam didn't have the heart left to join in any of the praising. I said to him, 'Don't worry. You're tired. You'll believe in it all again tomorrow.'

'What, you lot still here?' said the gatekeeper. 'Persistent little beggars, aren't you?'

Reluctantly, he led us round to a lean-to shelter built up against the bulk of the city wall.

'Suppose you better come in for the night.'

23

Bovine Breath

The shelter had a rusty tin roof and straw heaped on the floor. It was already overcrowded.

'Cows,' said the gatekeeper. 'Bishops' dairy herd. But they won't bother you.'

We were too tired to care. We lay down and slept almost at once. The big beasts' heavy breathing was comforting to hear. It kept us warm too.

We had to wake at dawn when the cowherd came to milk the cows. He gave us a bucketful to drink.

'Thank you,' I said.

'Don't thank me. Thank the gatekeeper. On his head be it. He said to help yourself to some of them crab apples too.' He pointed out a crooked little tree growing up beside the city wall.

The gatekeeper came to see us. 'Got a message from them inside. They're sending someone out to have a word with you lot. Don't say I didn't warn you.'

Two priests picked their way carefully through the mucky straw. The taller, meaner looking one was called the Dean. He was in charge.

'So which one of you's the leader of your gang?'

'We aren't a gang. But I suppose he is.' I pointed to Callam.

'No, him,' said Callam pointing to me.

'Well, it doesn't matter either way. The point is you can't any of you stay here. If the bishops' cows are disturbed, they won't milk properly.'

'Let us stay here. Please,' Callam said and he dropped to his knees at the Dean's feet. I thought he was going to kiss them. Both men looked embarrassed.

'You're our last hope. We've come a long way and we've nowhere else to go.'

'You should have thought of that before you set out.'

I said, 'Callam told me that your Lord says the poor shall inherit the earth and I think we're probably quite poor.'

The mean Dean sighed. 'He didn't intend it to be taken literally. It was a spiritual metaphor.'

'Besides,' the other priest interrupted, 'our Lord died over two thousand years ago. Things have changed. Nothing stays the same. *He* didn't set up the Mother Church.'

The Dean said, 'You dispossessed young people are all the same. It's absurd the way you spread these rumours among yourselves that this is a place of peace and plenty. Then you turn up here expecting us to perform miracles for you. Well, it can't be done!'

'The Dean is blessed with wisdom. He's got more than enough on his plate as it is. Running a place this size isn't easy for him, you know. It takes a lot of administration. There's no room for scroungers and hangers-on.'

I said, 'We don't want to be hangers-on. We want to be safe and work for our keep. All of us, don't we?'

The girl-mother nodded. 'I can cook. And sew.'

The blind boy said, 'I can knit.'

The Dean looked down at Tom, Dick, and John lolling sluglike about in the straw. 'And these?'

I said, 'They're really nice boys once you get to know them.'

'But what can they *do*?'

I remembered the SWU where nuts and screws were sorted. I said, 'I'm sure they want to work if something suitable's found for them and they're trained to it.'

'Pish,' said the Dean. 'I'm not an employment agent.

His holiness sent me out to resolve this business once and for all and that is what I intend to do.'

But shifting eleven exhausted children who don't want to be shifted isn't easy for two priests who don't want to get their robes dirty and don't like touching Dysfuncs with their bare hands.

They didn't manage to drag any of us even half-way back to the perimeter fence. They gave up and went away muttering to each other.

'Well, blimey,' the gatekeeper said. 'Gone and blown it for yourselves now. Tribunal hearing in the Chapter House. Discussing your case at their next meeting, that's what you've landed yourselves with.'

We had to wait five days to hear what the bishops decided. When you're waiting for bad news, time goes slowly. We rested up as much as we could and lived off cow's milk and sour little apples. Then Dick shambled off and got himself lost. When we found him he was sitting under a chute in the city wall, eating cold cooked meat. It was where the leftovers got thrown out. So that night we all ate quails' eggs and roast peacock for our supper.

The decision was reached. It was important. The Archbishop himself was to come out of the city and deliver it.

The gatekeeper was so alarmed that he made us wash our faces in the water trough, and lent us a wooden comb to tidy our hair. 'Don't say I didn't warn you he'd want to make an example of you,' he said mournfully.

A long procession of deacons and archdeacons, canons, acolytes, and all types of priests as well as singers, incense-swingers and candle-carriers, came twisting out through the big gates.

The tourists knew. There were more than usual, shoving each other aside to get a better view.

'Quick, on your knees, you lot, if you know what's good for you,' the gatekeeper whispered nervously as the Archbishop's palanquin was lowered to the ground.

Getting Tom, Dick, or John to do anything fast is a mistake. Tom began his rhythmic rocking. Dick made throaty roars of protest. John leaned over and began to chew my arm as a change from chewing his own. I managed not to cry out.

The Archbishop's hand drew aside the red satin curtain of his conveyance and he stepped down. The big cheese himself, in his silky red robes. He was small, round, and sweating. He looked nervous. He raised his hand for silence, adjusted the microphone, mumbled some prayer words even Callam couldn't understand, then began.

'When we view the numbers of feeble-minded who are finding their way to our sacred city in their sad escape from the inner city sectors, and their bid to avoid an early passing to peace, we know we are facing an almost insurmountable problem.'

As he spoke he stared just over our heads as though he couldn't bear to look any of us directly in the eyes.

'When we consider the menace they are to visiting foreigners, the threat they pose to hygiene, the air of degeneracy and misery they create as they cluster round our holy walls, we perceive that a proper solution must be reached.'

Callam was pressing his eyes tight shut, and clutching his hands together. His lips were moving. Either praying or wishing. Frankly, not much use in either.

'Previous theologians have been less liberal than we in their acceptance of these burdensome folk.' The Archbishop touched his gloved fingertips together and

125

gazed up into the sky, an even better way of not having to look at us. 'We now see they were misguided in their belief that Dysfunctionals, and all those of diminished responsibility, are necessarily evidence of Beelzebub's wicked ways and should be culled. We do not claim yet to understand what is their purpose in God's great order of things. However, we do feel that they should be preserved until such a time as their function is properly understood.'

I heard Callam let out a faint sigh of relief. So they definitely weren't going to SAD any of us.

'Henceforward, for every one of us ordained men who encounters any of these people in however slight a way, there are two things we must do. We must pray for them, that the Lord shall have mercy on them. And, more importantly, we must discourage all governments, worldwide, from exercising any presumed right to cull them.'

A grin of triumph from Callam.

But the Archbishop hadn't finished. He rolled his puffy eyes as though picking words carefully out of the clouds. He was sweating so much that parts of the satin on his robes were changing colour.

'However, to admit these unfortunates into the sacred heart of our community would create a precedent which might never be reversed, would create a mortal danger to the lives of our bishopric and their servants. For it is a known fact, conveyed to me by some of the wisest physicians in all the southern sectors whom my advisers have recently consulted, that one in four of all Dysfunctionals—and mongols such as these are no exception—have been guilty of various acts of violent behaviour.'

What's he on about? Dysfuncs aren't any more violent than anybody else! It all depends how they're treated. And as for DJLDSs, they're some of the gentlest, most affectionate people on earth. When John was biting me it wasn't malice but hunger.

I don't want to stay for the rest. I close my ears and try not to listen. But I can't block out the whining insistence of his voice.

I have to hear how he's going to build a special place where we can be housed. I have to hear the crowd applauding his decision.

'For the mental disability asylum,' he's saying, 'is the most blessed manifestation of true civilization any caring community can present. It has been, for some time, in our mind to construct just such an institution where all the unfortunates of life might be safely contained. For their own protection as much as that of others. Thanks be to God.'

Suddenly it's over. We're blessed with a quick wave of his hand. Then he steps back into his palanquin, draws the curtain, is lifted up and carried back into the city. The tourists record the receding procession with their cameras, then re-form in their queue.

DJLDSs may not be violent, but I am seething and in a mood for hitting somebody. 'Lies! All that stuff. What's he saying! He's a madman!'

Callam calms me down. 'Quit moaning. Just give thanks that we're no longer at risk. There's a roof over our heads and they're going to build us a nice home.'

Perhaps. There's just one detail that the venerable Archbishop didn't mention in his speech. To pay for the building of the asylum, we have to raise the funds ourselves. By begging. From tourist visitors.

Within the week, we become licensed beggars, each issued with our own beggar number, our own identification card. We must wear them on leather thongs around our necks. There are clear rules about how, where, and at what hours our begging must take place.

We're certificated to stand outside the great Westgate and nowhere else. No importuning at the helipad. No running up to visitors as they cross the gravel. We must look humble at all times. We may beg from foreign visitors only, not from any servant of the Mother Church or visiting priest.

Our begging boxes are secured with the Archbishop's own seal. On the seventh day of each week, they're collected up, opened, emptied, re-sealed and returned to us. The money is taken away to the Treasury for safe-keeping. We are never told how much there is. Sometimes, I doubt if we'll ever know.

But Callam says I must try to be more trusting. 'Where our treasure is, there will our hearts be also.'

What does he mean?

24

The Big Beyond

So we remain with the Mother Church, working away as beggars by day, scavenging for scraps in the evening, and always looking to the future day when there'll be enough money for them to start building our asylum.

But I don't know how much longer I can stick it. We've merely exchanged one kind of Low-Caste misery for another.

Callam tells me, 'Endure hardship as discipline.' He still clings to his mystic riddles even if he doesn't believe them any more.

'*I* don't mind the hardship. But what about poor Tom?' Sleeping on the hard filthy ground of the cowshed is giving him pressure sores.

Callam says, 'The foolishness of God is wiser than men. The weakness of God is stronger than men.'

'More riddles.'

'Listen, just quit moaning, brother. Give thanks we're saved.'

My body may have been saved but inside, I'm dying. It's the claustrophobia. All the people I once knew and tried to forget are coming back up to the surface, struggling for survival in my memory. There're so many. I'm suffocating from it. The thought of our dreary existence as beggars for the bishops going on for ever is unbearable.

'I keep thinking about Old Ma Peddle.'

'She was never your real mother. You told me so yourself. The church must be mother to you.'

He doesn't understand.

And beanpole Rah. And my sisters, Netta and Devon

and shouting Piccadilly. And Rah's Man. Did he and Pica make it here? Did they find it and get turned away?

Perhaps it's my own fault that I feel so alone. It doesn't make it any easier to bear.

I know I've got to move on. I tell Callam. He says, 'Then I suppose I better come with you.'

But I know he doesn't want to. 'No, please don't. You should stay. The boys need you.'

He tears me out some pages from the priest's notebook.

'The maps,' he says. They're hand-drawn and spidery like the writing. 'See, there's the safe-houses Father Gregory marked. You never know. They might still be OK to stay in.'

The gatekeeper gives me a satchel full of oatmeal.

'Scavvied,' he says with a wink. 'From the bishops' horses. I done it for the memory of my son.'

The bag's heavy. I find there's a gold chalice buried among the oats.

'Scavvied from the Treasury,' the gatekeeper says. 'Use it like money. In the pursuit of God's work. If I was younger, I'd come with you myself.'

At nightfall I'm ready. I embrace every one of the beggars, then my four brothers. Dick blinks with surprise, John gurgles and bites me. Tom lunges forward for a clumsy hug. Callam's too choked to say anything. I push my way through the standing cattle. Outside, my breath makes puffs in the early evening air.

And lurking in the shadows outside the shed is the tall blind boy. He's waiting for me.

'I want to come with you,' he says. He hooks his arm lightly on to mine. 'You'll need me to help you find the way. I can see in the dark.'

I don't believe him but I know I have to let him come too.

The gatekeeper is beckoning us across the gravel. He unlocks the outer perimeter fence for us.

And we're away.

I don't know where we're going. Will we find a way back across the river, head north towards the land of Rah's Man? Or will we walk over to the west, to find one of the New Age settlements that's willing to take us in?

Or perhaps misfits like us can't ever belong anywhere and have to keep roaming forever, till the end of our days.

ALSO BY RACHEL ANDERSON

Warlands

ISBN 0 19 271817 7

Once upon a time, quite a long time ago, in a beautiful faraway city where scarlet-flowering trees grew along wide streets, and where tropical sunsets reddened the evening skies, a small child was lying in the gutter . . .

When Amy goes to stay with her grandmother, she begs her to tell her stories about how Uncle Ho came to live with the family. Ho was a Vietnamese orphan, born amongst the bombings and terror of war, and the nightmares in his head are always with him.

No one really knows the true story of Ho's early life before he came to the family, but Amy's grandmother tells her the same stories she told Ho because, as her granny says, 'everyone needs to know the story of their life, even if it has to be invented.' And although the stories, like all good stories, start with 'Once upon a time,' Amy has to wait to find out if they will end with 'And they all lived happily ever after' . . .

The War Orphan

ISBN 0 19 275095 X

A helicopter appeared above the tree-tops of the forest.
    'Attention, people of this village! You are surrounded by Republic and allied forces. Stay where you are and await instructions. Do not run away or you will be shot!'

When Ha arrives as part of Simon's family, the nightmares arrive, too. And as Simon tries to find out about Ha and his past, he begins to uncover a war-story which is not the one he wanted to hear. Is the story Simon hears in his head his own, or does it belong to this child whom his parents now say is his brother—Ha, the war orphan?

Once, Simon had thought he was in control of his life. But as the story shifts its focus between himself and Ha, he grows more and more uncertain of his own identity. He becomes obsessed by the fascination, the horror, and the all-engulfing reality of total war.

'A rare and truthful book.'

Books for Your Children

'Compelling reading! . . . A beautiful, thought-provoking story, profoundly anti-war.'

ODEC: Books to Break Barriers

Paper Faces

ISBN 0 19 271614 X

Winner of the Guardian Children's Fiction Award

Dot didn't want anything to change. She'd had enough of that. Change was unsettling. It meant brick dust and disorder. The war was over and she was afraid.

May, 1945. Dot ought to be happy, but she isn't. Everything is changing, she's being moved from one place to another, and nothing is the same any more. Dot has to learn to cope with death, illness, and the return of the father who is a stranger to her. She begins to discover that there are different ways of looking at historical events, different kinds of truth, and many ways of being afraid and being brave.

'Rachel Anderson has written what is in one sense an historical novel, in another a profound study of self-discovery, and by any standards a rich and deeply moving story of childhood . . . The book is masterly in its control of narrative, but the reader is aware not of technical excellence but of understanding and tender, tough humour. This is a very fine book indeed.'

The Junior Bookshelf

The Doll's House

ISBN 0 19 271734 0

'Oh, wicked,' she sighed. It was a miniature house. She felt sure she'd seen it before. Then she realized it was one of those dream houses from inside her mind.

Becks, a rebellious young girl who won't go to school but dreams of her 'perfect house'; Patrick, a very ill teenager who has to stay in bed; Miss Amy Winters, an elderly spinster who looks back on her past and on a very special birthday present. Three very different people with something in common—the doll's house.

And then there are the dolls, who watch and wait but can never intervene.

'A thought provoking account of how three lives impinge . . . the really sensitive characterizations and strongly contrasted life styles grip and hold the attention.'

Spoken English